A hole shim...
adjacent ear...
and Fred ri...
an execut...
demon...

The hole stretched wider and it billowed, bulged. More little demons scampered out, and she and Cordy and O'Flaherty chopped and smashed at them as fast as they could. The horse had stopped screaming; she didn't dare look back in that direction. The more horrific sounds of tearing flesh and chewing were coming from that direction now. It was better to focus on Wes, who was steadily chanting, in Old Sumerian or Urdu. She hoped his buddy was keeping the demons off him long enough to let him finish the spell.

And quickly.

Fred looked up to see six hooked, shiny silver claws, each as long as the average scythe, slice through the portal's mist and curve around the edge of the hole, flexing as if to get a better grip on reality. Her reality.

Angel™

Available from Pocket Books

ANGEL ™

book of the dead

Ashley McConnell

**An original novel based on the television series
created by Joss Whedon & David Greenwalt**

POCKET
BOOKS

London   New York   Sydney   Toronto

Historian's Note: This book takes place in the fourth season of *Angel*.

First Pocket Books edition August 2004
Text copyright © 2004 Twentieth Century Fox
Pocket Books
An imprint of Simon & Schuster
Africa House, 64–78 Kingsway
London WC2B 6AH
www.simonsays.co.uk

Printed and bound in Great Britain by
Cox & Wyman Ltd, Reading, Berkshire

First edition 10 9 8 7 6 5 4 3 2 1

A CIP catalogue record for this book is available from the British Library

ISBN 0-7434-9234-X

ACKNOWLEDGMENTS

The author would like to thank Tricia Boczkowski for the opportunity, Jennifer Jackson and Patrick Price for their patience in their respective roles, and the Blue Fish for once again proving the adage that friends are the family you find. Chicken Little is beginning to discover that the sky is not, in fact, always falling.

CHAPTER ONE

"Oh, look," said the hated voice over his shoulder. "Here's Emilio Herrera, scientist extraordinary. That doesn't look much like a sketch of meiosis, Emilio. Why don't we show it to the rest of the class and see what they think?"

Emilio squirmed down deeper in his seat and put his hands over the drawing. "No, I—"

"Oh, but you must." Gina Grey slapped her ruler on the back of his chair. The loud *thwack* made him jump, and somehow the picture that had been under his protecting hands wasn't there anymore, and Ms. Grey was holding it up for all the class to see. "Look, boys and girls. Does this look like meiosis to you?"

Emilio always sat in the back of the room because it felt safer not to have people behind him, poking him, watching him, talking about him where he couldn't see. Now that meant every person in the class was turning around in his or her seat to stare and giggle while Ms. Grey held his work up in front of her skinny chest and rotated, making sure everybody got a good look.

"That looks like dragons," Deborah piped up.

Ms. Grey held it up for a moment longer while a murmur of agreement rose, and then turned the picture around to give it an ostentatious examination. "Why, Deborah, I think you might be right. It does look sort of like a dragon."

"I think it looks like a cow with a hangover," said Tim Markowitz, from the jocks' corner of the classroom. His buddies sniggered and nudged one another. Tim wore a letter jacket all the time, even when it was a hundred degrees outside.

"Yes, it could be a cow," Ms. Grey agreed. "Which is it, Emilio? A dragon? Or a cow?"

It's you, he wanted desperately to say. *It's a picture of you, you bitch.* The sketch featured fangs and horns and claws, ripping at something. He hadn't had a chance to put in the school yet. That would be just a box in the background, anyway. Why waste time drawing the school when he could spend hours getting just the right shading on the evil eyes or the scaly hide or the wings.

"Are you going to answer me, Emilio?" Ms. Grey taunted.

He shook his head and shrank deeper.

"Well, then, we don't know what this is, class. But we're all pretty sure this isn't a picture of a cell dividing, aren't we?"

A ragged chorus of assent, salted with laughter.

"And we're studying dividing cells today. Not dragon cows. Is this an Art assignment, Emilio?"

He wanted desperately to say, *Yes, it's homework, give it back.*

"I'm in Art," Shirley, Deborah's twin sister, said importantly. "Emilio's not in Art this year. Besides, we're not doing stupid dragon cows in Art, either! We're doing soft sculpture this semester."

"Oooh," Ms. Grey said, as if enlightened. "So this isn't schoolwork at all."

The class grinned at one another, knowing what was coming next.

"Well then, it doesn't belong here, does it?" With a sharp jerk of her wrists, she tore the drawing in half, and then in half again, across the face of the portrait. She continued ripping until the picture was in confetti pieces, and then opened her hands and let them fall around his head in a little rain of paper. Slapping her hands smartly against each other, she leaned over and whispered in Emilio's ear, loud enough for the guys in front and on either side of him to hear, "Do that again in my classroom, little boy, and you'll lose more than a drawing. Kids get suspended these days for making up violent pictures, you know that?"

And with that, she marched up to the front of the class and started talking about stupid meiosis again.

After class, he made his way to his locker, his eyes still burning with embarrassment. That was probably why he didn't see the girl standing there, right in front of his locker, talking with her stupid friends. He practically walked into her.

"Watch it, you freak," she said to him. Then she went on to her gaggle of friends as if he couldn't hear, "Frankenstein much?"

"Oh no, that's Emilio. He's Rain Man. I bet if you dropped toothpicks he'd count them."

"Not Emilio! He can't count that high!"

They moved on down the hallway, laughing. He fumbled with the combination to his locker, pretending he was deaf.

"Excuse *me*," an impatient voice behind him snapped. "Could you do the makeout with your locker some other time? Some of us need to get to class."

It was Victoria Jensen, whose locker was the one just below his. They were always getting in each other's way at class change time.

"What on, Victers?" It was Markowitz, swaggering toward the lockers, his fists shoved deep into the pockets of the jacket to make sure the letter was more obvious. Three of his friends from the B string wrestling team were with him. "Is Mealy here giving you bad sitch?"

Victoria gave her knights-errant an exasperated look. "Go away, Markowitz. I don't need you Arnolding in here."

"I'm not Arnold," Tim said, injured. "I'm Rockin'. See?"

He shoved at Emilio, who was pulling a backpack out of his locker. The strap snagged and pivoted him into the wall. The back of the locker door hit the next locker with a loud *clang* that attracted even more attention. As if he needed it.

"Come on, Mealyworm. Stand up to it."

He ignored the other boy, turning around to unhook his backpack strap from the locker door. Sometimes ignoring worked.

Sometimes it didn't. "What's the matter, Mealy?" Tim turned to the open locker. "You got more dragon cows in there? Let's see." His cronies laughed. Encouraged, he grabbed the back of Emilio's shirt and pulled hard to get him out of his way. The neckline hem came up against his throat, and Emilio choked.

The two-minute buzzer sounded.

"Markowitz, will you get out of my way," Victoria said, as annoyed now at the jocks as she was at Emilio. "I'm trying to get to class on time for a change."

"Oh, *sorry*," Tim said, making an elaborate show of stepping back and giving Victoria room. "We wouldn't want Victers to be late for class, would we?"

Emilio snatched the opportunity to slam his locker shut and twist the combination dial. Outraged, Markowitz reached for him again, twisting his hand into the front of his shirt. The frayed material ripped under his hands.

"Aren't you supposed to be in class?" It was one of the teachers from the History pod, making his way down the hall and herding students before him. He paused by the locker, pointedly watching until Markowitz let go and shrugged.

"Sure," he said. "I was just helping Emilio here clean out his locker. We'll finish it up after school, won't we?" His ugly stare promised that he had more than cleaning out a locker in mind.

The teacher could see what was going on. He didn't care. His job was to clear out the hallways by the time class started, and the final bell for the next period was ringing now. "I think you'd better get moving or I'm going to be handing out detentions to all of you," he said.

Victoria gave an indignant, if futile, protest. Markowitz and his buddies grinned at one another and swaggered off, with a pointed "See you later, Mealy-o!"

With most of the kids taken care of, the teacher glanced at Emilio and decided he wasn't worth the further hassle. "Get to class," he said, and went on down the hallway, leaving him standing with the canvas backpack hanging by its straps from his hands.

His next class was California History, the one he'd had to take because Art had already filled up by the time he'd arrived to register. He hated California History.

Without actually deciding, he walked down the hall, his backpack swinging from his hand, and instead of turning right at the end to his classroom, he turned left. That way led to the front lobby of the school, where the glass trophy cases stood, the banners for school elections still hung from the ceiling, casting shadows on the image of a shark painted on the concrete floor, and the front door waited, leading outside. Away from all this.

It was an omen, he decided, when a rare city bus pulled up just as he got to the street. And another omen that he had exact change in his pocket for the fare. He accepted a transfer without really intending to, and threw himself in one of the seats, looking around.

There was a druggie in the back, sleeping it off. Two Hispanic women were talking to each other in a rapid-fire stream of Spanish, which he didn't understand a word of despite two years of class. They had shopping bags stacked at their feet, and when they saw him looking, they pulled the bags a little closer. There was a black guy in a suit, reading something from a briefcase, and another black guy, listening to music through headphones, swaying and mouthing the lyrics. Emilio was the only

7

teenager on the bus. He wondered if the driver would get in trouble for picking him up from school in the middle of the day. Who cared what he did, after all? Mr. Lines didn't even take roll in History class half the time, anyway.

He sat through four stops, watching as the guy with the briefcase got off in front of an insurance building and two more druggies got on—white ones this time—and the Hispanic shopper ladies gathered up all their bags and held them in their laps to protect them. They got off two stops later.

He was now in a part of town he didn't recognize at all. As the bus came to yet another stop, engine wailing, hydraulics sighing as the doors slid open, he stood up and got off, still clutching the transfer. The driver gave him a funny look as the bus pulled away and left him, and he realized he was in the middle of a block. No transfers here. He let the strip of yellow paper go, watching as it fluttered in the breeze, tumbled along the sidewalk, and finally came to rest against a shop door.

This whole street was mom-and-pop establish-ments, huddled up to the street in a row, a strip mall for people too broke to go to the real stores, he thought. There was a lunch place that featured Tacos To Go, a shoe place promising deep dis-counts, and even a storefront church with a big cross on the outside; across the street and down a little ways was a boarded-up movie theater. A handful of pedestrians walked past. He considered getting a taco, burrito maybe, but he wasn't really hungry. Down by the corner, a guy was holding up a sign: HOMELESS. PLES HELP. Even his mom wouldn't want to live down here. And his dad, well . . . not even. His dad was too worried about what they'd think of him at the office.

The transfer was still tagged to the shop door, fluttering. As if it were beckoning to him. He stepped back to look at the name of the place, inscribed in chipped and fading paint over the picture window. BEYOND THE VEIL, it said.

The stuff in the window looked like a cross between an antique store and a bookstore: a three-legged table with a large crystal ball resting on a brocade drape; some Days of the Dead paintings of a skeletal jazz trio, complete with piano and trumpet; another table, low and long, with a display of books among an apparently random collection of rocks; a brass dragon incense burner; a wicked-looking knife; and a really cool sword.

What the hell. He didn't have anyplace else he needed to be.

He followed the invitation, pausing only to look at the name of the store painted again on the front glass in elaborate script, this time with the owner's name prominently featured: CAWBER'S BEYOND THE VEIL. There were more words, but they were scratched to the point of unreadability.

"Hello, can I help you?" said a cheerful voice from behind the front counter. It was an old man—really old, maybe fifty—with a circle of gray hair around a bald skull, and wire-rimmed glasses shoved up firmly against his face. There was nobody else in the place, and the old guy had been sitting reading a book.

"No, I'm just lookin'."

"Go right ahead. If you need anything, give me a shout." The guy smiled and went back to his book without another look.

There was lots to look at, it turned out. He first thought the place was just a bookstore, but the front counter had glass cases full of stuff: crystal balls, little brass bowls stacked with cones of incense no longer than the first joint of his thumb, funny-looking wood carvings, medals without patron saints on them, obsidian flaked blades and arrowheads. There was a lot of jewelry, too, mostly silver with pink-and-white quartz, onyx, and some vivid green malachite. He remembered the names from his Geology class last year. He'd liked Geology.

He wandered along the counter, looking, his knapsack still hanging, banging against his legs.

Someone came in behind him. He looked up to see a tall man with glasses looking across the counter at the shelves full of books.

"Mr. Wyndam-Pryce! It's been quite some time!" The old man sounded like this was somebody he knew pretty well, and liked. Emilio watched out of the corner of his eye as the two men talked head to head, dark hair by gray, as the old man pulled out several books and the two of them paged through them.

The younger guy didn't buy anything, but the old man didn't seem to be disappointed. "I'll certainly look out for that," he said happily. "It'll be fun to track it down."

The other man smiled and turned to go. He glanced at Emilio as he left, nodded politely as their eyes met, and went away.

The old man put the books away, smiling vaguely at Emilio as he did so. Emilio thought he must keep the happy act for his regular customers.

A little cream-colored rectangular block, deeply carved, caught his eye. He couldn't tell what it was, looking down at it, so he crouched to get a better angle. He still couldn't tell.

"Would you like to take a closer look?" the old man asked. He put away the last book and came over, unlocking the glass case. He reached in and picked up the little figure and set it on a square of black velvet cloth he'd produced from somewhere. Emilio picked the little object up to examine it. It wasn't even two inches long. He could see traces of bright blue and green coloring in the fissures.

"It's a netsuke," the old man said. "It's Japanese. Real ivory, maybe a hundred and fifty years old."

"Cool." He had no idea what a "net-ski" was, but it was really old, and that intrigued him. He turned it over and over in his fingers, trying to figure out what it was supposed to represent. "It's got holes in the back."

"That was where they hung it from the sash—belt," explained the old man patiently, off Emilio's blank look. "The Japanese used these to weight down their sashes to keep them from flying all over the place."

"Cool," Emilio said again, hefting it in his hand. It wasn't heavy at all, for something that was supposed to be a weight. And it seemed like the happy act wasn't just for the regulars. The guy was actually friendly, and not in a creepy way, either. "What *is* it?"

"It's a coiled-up dragon. See, he's got one paw covering his eyes. He's peeking out." The old man's voice was getting enthusiastic as he pointed out the detail. Emilio couldn't help grinning back at him, and then looking at the block again. Sure enough, now that he knew what to look for, he could see that the carving was a coiled body.

"He's got no wings," Emilio pointed out.

"That kind of dragon doesn't have wings."

"There's different kinds? I didn't know that." For some reason, admitting he didn't know was easy. This guy wasn't going to make fun of him because he didn't know.

He looked more closely at the delicate claws covering the dragon's face.

The dragon's eyes flashed green.

"Oh, wow! How cool!"

"What is it?" the old man said.

"Where does the battery go? I can't see it. Or I bet it's got a chip inside."

"I don't think so," the man said doubtfully. "What do you mean?"

"Didn't you see it? The eyes flash at you. Look." He put the little thing back on the display cloth so the storekeeper could see. But now the eyes were blank, almost invisible behind the claws.

"They flashed? Really? It's never done that for me."

"How much is this?"

The old man smiled at him. "This? It's a pretty expensive piece. This could go in a museum." He picked up the netsuke and placed it on the palm of his hand, studying it. "The eyes never flashed before. What color were they?"

"Green. Real bright. Like emeralds. Are you sure you didn't see?" The disappointment was thick in his throat. If it was expensive—and Emilio believed him; the old guy didn't seem like he was just trying to up the price on him—he couldn't afford it. He could barely afford to download for his iPod.

"No, I never did. Green, you say. How strange.

You'd think a dragon's eyes would be red, wouldn't you?" The old man sighed, and then brightened. "Maybe you'd like to look at some of the other things over here." He slipped the little block into his pocket and led Emilio over to a six-foot-tall glass case behind a little reading nook with a couple of overstuffed chairs and a small table stacked with books.

Opening the case, he took out a small, dark green, oval stone. It was maybe an inch and a half long, not quite an inch wide; it was divided in half, and then one of the two sides was divided again, lengthwise. The oblong stone was set in gold, the lines on its surface filled in with gold. "This is an Egyptian scarab," he said, placing it in Emilio's hand so he could feel the heft of it. "A scarab is a beetle. The ancient Egyptians believed that scarab beetles rolled the sun across the sky. They used them extensively in their magical workings."

"Magic?" Emilio said. This guy was awfully trusting, he thought. There was nothing to keep him from knocking the old man down and taking all the stuff out of this cabinet. It was probably worth a fortune.

Except Emilio wasn't a threat, and the guy could sense that. Besides, it was a lot more interesting to hear him talk. Lots more interesting than Biology or California History.

"Magic," the old man confirmed. "Real magic, not like sitting in a box starving yourself for a month."

"Yeah, what was that about?" Emilio agreed. "That's not magic, that's just sitting there not eating."

No one else came in all afternoon, and the shadows lengthened while they talked. The old man was Cawber, the owner of the store. Cawber pulled out all kinds of amulets and things and explained what they were, and took books off the shelf to show him they were really old, not just fakes. They sat in the reading nook, and Cawber talked about the old times—the spells and stuff that sorcerers made. And some of them, he promised, really worked.

Emilio believed him. He traced the words in the books, at least the words in English, because a lot of the books were written in other languages, and some even in characters like Japanese, and there was one where all the letters were tiny pictures. He told Cawber about the picture of the dragon he had drawn in Biology class, and what happened to it, and Cawber was indignant for him. The old guy was interesting and funny and he *listened* to what Emilio had to say, never talked down to him, even when he was explaining stuff that was so easy once Emilio understood what he was getting at.

It wasn't until the neon cross on the church came on, glaring into the store window, that either one of them realized how late it was.

ANGEL

"Oh my goodness," Cawber said, and it didn't sound silly coming from him. "I'm afraid you'd better be getting home, young man."

"Yeah, I guess so." Emilio got up with reluctance, fumbling for his backpack.

Cawber hesitated, and then said, "It's not safe after dark."

Emilio shrugged. He knew that. Everybody knew that.

"If you have a problem—well, there's something you can say. It's not a big thing, but it might help."

"A magic thing?"

Cawber smiled bashfully. "A little thing of my own. It's what we call a 'cantrip.' A really little spell. It works sometimes."

"Yeah?"

"You say, 'Ice and fire, reflect evil ire; earth and air, keep all things fair; *los deseos malvados, salen.*'"

Emilio mouthed the words. "That's it?"

Cawber shrugged. "Like I said, it's not a big thing. If you haven't got the power, it's just a silly rhyme and a wish in Spanish. But what harm can it do?"

"Yeah, I guess."

Cawber looked out the window and waved his hand at the window as if to wipe dust off it, although it was at least a yard away from him. "It looks like your bus is coming. I hope I'll see you again soon."

"Hey, I'd like that." He looked out into the street, which was still empty. *What bus?* he thought. "I guess you need to close up and stuff."

"I'm afraid so. Go on now, you don't want to miss the bus. Don't forget your transfer." Cawber gently shooed him out the door and into the night. He found himself standing on the sidewalk, looking back into the store as the lights went out, and shivered as a couple of cars slowed as they went by. He found himself muttering the words Cawber had given him. The panhandler had given up, he thought. He hoped.

"Los deseos malvados, salen," he said, practicing. Only practicing.

And a moment later, there was the bus, the doors sighing open for him.

He handed the driver the yellow transfer.

Wasn't this on the ground outside? he wondered abruptly. He remembered distinctly seeing the slip of paper sticking to the glass of the door. How had the old man gotten it? But the driver took it without comment, and Emilio took a seat in the empty bus and rode it back to school. From there, he could catch another bus back home. Not the school bus, of course. It was too late for that, and besides, only losers rode school buses.

He missed dinner. His father wasn't home from work yet, but his mother had already put everything away, and his little sister was sitting at the kitchen

17

table studying math, the boots and hat from her riding lesson on the floor beside her. He tried the cantrip.

"What did you say?" Eloisa said. She showed absolutely no signs of picking her stuff up and going away. Well, maybe she wasn't a *deseos malvados*. She was only eleven, after all.

His mother, standing in the kitchen doorway, sighed. "There's no point in asking you where you were, is there? Where were you?"

He shrugged. "Out. Doing stuff."

This kind of answer, as he well knew, usually resulted in his mother yelling at him, him yelling back, and Eloisa running back to her bedroom crying. He couldn't think of anything else to say, though. He sure wasn't going to tell her he cut school. She'd tell his dad, and his dad would give him another long lecture about how he had to study or he'd never make it into law school.

This time, though, his mother just raised a hand and dropped it again, and went back out into the living room.

Eloisa let go a pent-up breath.

Emilio shrugged again and got out some cold pizza from the night before. It might have been the old man's cantrip. It might not. He was just glad not to get yelled at.

Although if it *was* the cantrip, that was pretty cool.

CHAPTER TWO

The next morning, Emilio hurried to school, hoping to get into his locker and into his homeroom class without running into Victoria or, worse, Markowitz.

It was too much to hope for.

His arm was twisted behind his back in fine TV-cop style, and his face was smushed into the locker door. "You little pig," Markowitz growled into his ear. "I was looking for you yesterday. You think you can hide from me?"

Emilio yelped as his arm was forced higher. It felt like his shoulder was going to pop right out of its socket. He tried dropping down to relieve the pressure, but Markowitz—a second-string wrestler—was ready.

"I'm gonna pound you into the ground," Markowitz said into his ear. "I'm gonna rip your arm right off." For emphasis, he jerked the arm again, and Emilio screamed. Out of the corner of his eye, Emilio saw other students, some of them staring at them, some of them carefully not. He tried to remember the cantrip, but it hurt too much to concentrate.

"Yo, Tim," one of the other jocks said. "Teacher coming!"

The pressure on Emilio's arm lessened fractionally while Markowitz said, "Head her off. I'm not done here."

"Ice and . . . and fire, reflect evil ire . . . ," Emilio gasped. What was the rest of it? "Earth and air, keep all things fair!"

"What?" Markowitz dropped Emilio's arm, spun him around, and slammed him back into the lockers. Emilio's head rang with the impact against the metal. "Are you talking to me, you little jerk?"

What the *hell* was the rest of it—it was in Spanish; he didn't speak Spanish. Nobody in his family spoke Spanish. Nobody but Eloisa, who was taking a beginner's course. He opened his eyes to see Markowitz leaning into him. The words rushed out. "Ice and fire, reflect evil ire; earth and air, keep all things fair; *los deseos malvados, salen*," he chanted. *"Los deseos malvados, salen!"*

Tim Markowitz let go of his shirt and stepped back, a confused look in his eyes. "Huh?"

"Ice and fire, reflect evil ire; earth and air, keep all things fair; *los deseos malvados, salen*," Emilio repeated, his heart beating loudly in his ears.

"Okay, okay," the bully said. "You don't have to shout."

And he turned and walked away.

Emilio watched him go, his jaw hanging.

"*What* did you say to him?" Victoria demanded. "I thought he was going to Bruce Lee you."

"So did I," Emilio whispered, rubbing his sore arm.

That afternoon, Emilio cut California History again and went back to Cawber's—the first of many afternoons.

Now that he had the cantrip, Emilio discovered that he didn't have to be afraid of Markowitz anymore. He caught the bully looking at him, sometimes, with a puzzled expression on his face, but he always seemed to find something else to do instead of threaten Emilio.

"It works that way sometimes," Cawber said, when Emilio later described the situation. "If someone really doesn't have any reason to do bad things to you, they'll forget they were doing them. You can't depend on it all the time, though." He was always saying that, reminding him not to depend on all the little spells and workings he was teaching him. They weren't dependable, he said. If you depended on them, they'd stop working for you right when you needed them most.

That was the day that the big box came in with no return address. It was heavy—the shipping guy

21

grunted when he dumped it on the counter. Emilio signed for it since Cawber was busy with a customer who wanted a particular kind of dried herb.

"Tobey?" Emilio was still getting used to calling Cawber by his first name. "You want me to unpack this?" he asked.

"Who's it from?" The old guy always wanted to know before he'd let Emilio open a box. Emilio figured that he was making sure there was nothing dangerous first. That was fine with him.

"Doesn't say."

"Well, that's strange. Let's wait until I can open it with you, okay?"

It was really late before all the customers were gone. The old man was tired, Emilio could tell, but he closed up the shop and set the box on the floor back in the reading nook. "Let's see what we've got here."

Before applying the box cutter, he set his hands on the cardboard. He was trying to get the vibrations, Emilio knew; he could do that, too, a little, now. At first Cawber didn't say anything, his face perfectly blank. Then he smiled. "Well, I think this is going to be pretty interesting."

The box contained old books. Some were mildewed and falling apart, and the old man tsk'd with disapproval, setting those aside. The remainder looked fragile; many of them without titles on the spine, because the lettering had rubbed off over the years, Cawber explained.

Emilio was disappointed not to find anything more interesting in the shipment. Sure, some books held spells, containing pretty powerful stuff. A few books in the back room even had summoning spells. He wasn't quite sure *what* would be summoned, but from the way the customers treated the books, it had to be something pretty powerful. The old guy never sold those books, no matter how much he was offered. He'd let people look at them, and sometimes copy out a few things, but that was all. Emilio asked to look at them—he wanted to try one out to see what would happen—but Cawber always needed something more pressing done first. It was weeks before Emilio figured out that it was all just a nice way of telling him he wasn't allowed.

Cawber stacked eight or nine of the old books and carried them into the back room, where he had his office. While he did so, Emilio glanced at the rest. Yes, at least one of these things must have summoning spells.

On impulse, he shoved a random book into his backpack. Cawber hadn't cataloged the shipment yet. There wasn't any packing slip. He'd never know one was missing, and Emilio was going to bring it back once he had tried out some stuff. It wasn't like he was a thief.

"I should be getting home," Emilio called.

Standing outside the front door as the storekeeper

locked up, Emilio wondered for the first time if Cawber had any kind of a life outside the little shop. He couldn't recall ever seeing him set foot outside before. The older man looked up and down the street a long time, particularly at the streetlamp that had burned out.

"Emilio," he said at last, "you've been such a great help to me, and you stay a lot later than you should. I haven't been able to pay you, but I want you to know how much I appreciate everything you do for me."

"Hey, it's nothing," Emilio started to say, but the old man had already dug deep into his pocket and was holding out his hand.

"This is supposed to be yours, I think," Cawber said. "From the first time you looked at it. Why don't you take it?"

It was the little ivory netsuke.

"Wow," he stammered. He had a better idea, now, how much this little figurine was worth; he'd heard customers bargaining for similar examples. "I couldn't—"

"Of course you could. Don't be silly. The eyes never flashed for me, you know."

The weight of the thing was cool in his palm, and as he looked down at the coy little dragon peeking at him through its claws, he saw those eyes shining green at him.

He swallowed. "Oh—okay. Thanks, Mr. Cawber."

"I told you to call me Tobey, now didn't I?" the old man said gently. "Here's your bus. On your way, then."

Emilio spent a long time looking out the back window of the bus, watching, as Tobey Cawber trudged steadily down the street in the opposite direction. Every night Cawber walked to a local diner for dinner; he'd told Emilio that that way he didn't have to cook in the little apartment over the store. He kept on looking until the old man turned a corner and was out of sight. And all that time the little dragon was coiled, a cool comforting lump, in his hand.

Emilio took the book of spells to school with him, and sneaked it open in Biology class. It was written in English, but the spelling was really funny, and the print was thick and dark and hard to read. The pages crackled as he turned them. Mrs. Grey gave him a sharp look, but she was too busy with some girls who didn't want to cut into a dead rabbit. Turning back to the book, he sat and read, mouthing the unfamiliar words.

Class was nearly over before Mrs. Grey got around to marching over. He looked up in time to see her reaching for his book, and automatically he said his protection cantrip.

It didn't work. Her long, bony hands never hesitated.

Emilio yanked the book back and stood up, facing her.

"Mr. Herrera, give me that book right now."

"It's mine," he said. "You can't have it."

"Right *now*, I said!" And she reached for it again.

Emilio repeated the spell he'd just been reading as he stepped back.

Across town, in the Hyperion Hotel, Cordelia Chase, Angel Investigations' conduit to the Powers That Be, stiffened. "Oh, damn," she said.

"What is it?" Angel asked. "Are you having another vision?"

Cordy had come a long way from being the Queen Bitch of Sunnydale High. Her visions were a big part of that—they were a responsibility she had never asked for, and never wanted, but they provided her purpose in life. Her visions were of people in trouble—supernatural, demonic trouble—and they were a heads-up that often allowed Angel and his friends to save lives. Still, she was never going to actually *enjoy* them.

"Hoo boy, I'll say." She rubbed hard at her temples. While the visions no longer carried the threat of death for Cordelia, who had been made part demon by the Powers That Be, they still took her by surprise. Doyle, the original channel for mystical IMing, had described it as a "splitting headache," and he was legitimately half-demon. "We got a kid, it looks like, in school. High school, going Carrie, only he's a boy. He's—it looks like he's summoning something."

"Where?"

Cordelia concentrated. "In a lab class?"

"What *school*?" said Angel.

Cordelia shook her head. For somebody who had been around for centuries, Angel could be awfully impatient. "Well, if The PTB sent me these things with labels, I could tell you. All I know is, it's a kid, in a lab—I could see those long tables and sinks, and Bunsen burner-y stuff. He's young, and he wears something around his neck on a string. And he's really mad."

"That's not a big help." Angel was a vampire, but unlike the vampires and other demonic denizens that he hunted, he had a soul. He had a lot of death to make up for over the course of his long life, and he didn't much like vague messages that got in his way of doing that.

"I could look on the Web for local schools," Fred offered.

While Cordelia Chase was Angel Investigations' conduit to the Powers That Be, Winifred Burkle—otherwise known as Fred—was their primary scientific resource. She did all the technical and technological research and analysis for the group—and recently, she'd been doing her best in the paranormal and occult research areas as well, even though her background was in physics and math. A slight, shy brunette, she was less vivid, maybe, than the forthright Cordelia, but she was lovely too.

"Yeah, but that won't tell us which one is being invaded from another dimension," Gunn reminded her. "Looks like we're going to have to wait for the evening news for that." Charles Gunn had fought vampires on the streets of Los Angeles for years, with his own team of some of the toughest street fighters in Los Angeles. He was a part of Angel Investigations because Angel's friends were the most efficient, most accomplished players in the game. With Cordelia's line of communication to The Powers, they had an advantage over everybody else. Gunn was up for every advantage he could get.

Sure enough, a report on the evening news described an explosion and fire in one of the science laboratories at Northeast Burbank Union High School. "No fatalities," the announcer said—with disappointment? "The only injuries were suffered by one of the teachers as she led her class out of the room. The damage is estimated at nearly half a million dollars."

"Whoa," Gunn said. "That was a kid with a mad on."

"He sure was," Cordelia said. "I'm afraid we're going to hear from him again. The PTB doesn't send me these vision things for my health."

"Was he the only one involved?" Angel asked. "What are we dealing with here?"

"I couldn't tell," Cordy admitted. "But he was throwing around some pretty powerful magic."

"Well, let's find out before he—or they—decide to take out more than a high school science lab, okay?" Angel's frustration was obvious. There just wasn't enough to work on—not yet.

"I can check out the school, see if I can find out who was involved," Fred offered. Her fingers were already flying over the keyboard.

Three days later, when the school finally reopened, Emilio realized nobody in his Biology class was going to tell the police anything. Well, Mrs. Grey tried—repeatedly—but she was in the hospital being treated for "minor burns and shock," and nobody was listening to her raving. It was nice, though, hearing the rumors fly through the school. One or two even named him, and people started giving him a wide berth. It was a powerful rush, getting that kind of respect. He wondered if Tobey Cawber could do this kind of stuff, and if so, why he was still running that junky little shop. He wondered if his customers could do this stuff. That guy who had been in the store the first day—Wyndam-Pryce—had been back a couple of times. He didn't look like he could do much.

But then, neither did Emilio. Sometimes appearances were deceiving. He grinned to himself. His classmates edged away.

A week went past before he could get away from his worried mother long enough to return to Cawber's. He prepared a story for Tobey in case the old man asked questions. He didn't want to tell him what had *really* happened in his Biology class. He had an idea Tobey Cawber wouldn't be very happy about that.

But he didn't need a story. The store was locked and dark when he arrived. Looking through the windows, he couldn't see any movement inside.

He glanced up and down the street before trying a new spell he'd found in the book—one guaranteed to open any door, unstick anything stuck. And it worked. He slipped inside the store, closing the door behind him. "Tobey?" he called out. "Are you here?"

There was no answer.

The place was spooky-silent. Reluctantly, he walked through, looking the place over.

Nothing.

He went into the back room to Cawber's office. A pile of books on the desk looked familiar—they'd come from that box, the one with no return address. A half-full cup of coffee sat beside them. It was cold, with a skim over the top and a light coating of dust sitting on the liquid. Emilio looked around quickly, convinced he had heard someone at the door, but there was no one. A book lay open on the floor beside the chair, as if it had been dropped by someone in a hurry. Cawber didn't treat books that way. He picked it up, closing it carefully, and then paused.

He really, really wanted to read this book, he realized. He *really* wanted to. It was an important book, full of things he ought to know. It *thrummed* to him, more than any of the other books he'd handled in the store.

But Cawber had been reading it. He couldn't take it; the old man would miss it. He felt guilty enough as it was, accepting the little dragon figure when borrowing—his dad would say "wrongfully taking"—the other book. That was the same as stealing, only Emilio's dad couldn't say anything that simple.

He dropped the big dark book unopened on the desk, wiping his hands on his jeans, and looked at the other volumes.

Okay, if he couldn't take the one Cawber was reading, why not one of these?

Or two? Or—

But his eyes kept being drawn back to Cawber's reading selection. What was inside? He *really* wanted to know. And it *wasn't* wrongful taking, any more than checking something out of a library was. He was going to bring them back.

Suddenly afraid of the unbroken silence, he snatched up several of the books on Cawber's desk—maybe they weren't as strong, but they talked to him too—shoved them into his backpack, and ran through the store to the front. He was out the door, looking for the bus, when he saw a police cruiser turn down the street. That was all he'd need, getting caught by the cops outside an open door to an empty store. His dad would have a cow.

He whispered the spell reversal and then turned away, as if he'd just tried the door and found it locked. The cruiser slowed beside him as he walked down the sidewalk, wondering where the bus was—it had always shown up for him whenever he'd left the store before.

The cops were eyeing him.

He whispered the cantrip for you-don't-see-me.

The cruiser pulled away.

The next day at school, Victoria approached him at his locker as he was stowing away Cawber's "borrowed" books. The little dragon, now held to his chest on a rawhide cord, warmed up noticeably.

"Hey, Emilio. What's up?"

He looked at her disbelievingly. Why would Victoria be interested in him? "Nothing," he replied. He lifted the dragon away from his skin. It felt so hot, it should have burned him, but it was still cool against his fingers.

"What are those?" She pointed to the books. "They look pretty old."

He was seized by a desire to shock her. "They're magic. Books of spells."

Instead of blowing him off, she nodded thoughtfully. "I thought so," she said. "You're messing with some pretty heavy stuff, aren't you?"

She knew!

"Yeah," he said. "Pretty heavy."

"What kinds of things can you do?"

He grinned. "Want to come with me after school and see?"

"Where?"

He thought fast. He hadn't really considered where else he could experiment on big stuff. Then he remembered Markowitz talking to his friends about his new job at a movie theater. He'd offered to get them in free, but he'd sneered at Emilio. "I know a place."

"Can I bring some friends?"

He bared his teeth in something like a grin. "Yeah, sure. Let's invite Markowitz."

Three hours later, at the Hyperion Hotel, Cordelia got another vision.

CHAPTER THREE

"It's the damned Tovateir demons," Gunn said. "Man, I hate those things." He balanced a crowbar in his left hand and crouched slightly, balancing on the balls of his feet. Behind him, Fred pulled a fairly useless stake out of her sleeve. She would have brought a wakizashi, but she didn't have a long coat, and anyway, it was hard to hide a blade nearly two feet long on your person when you weren't much more than five feet tall to begin with. Stakes didn't work with Tovateirs. You had to squish them, or knock their grinning heads off.

And they *would* keep grinning—lips peeled back from great big teeth, flat dark eyes crinkled into tiny little slits, and piles and piles of wiry brown-green fur on top of nine-feet-tall angular bodies. And then there were those long, clutchy arms and razor-sharp green nails. The nails were the worst part, because they were also deadly poisonous.

The Tovateir demons hung out in packs, five and six at a time. Fred and Gunn picked the wrong alley to walk past, and now a whole herd of demons poured out to surround them, grabby nails clicking and teeth snapping.

"Remind me to pick a different theater for the late-night movie next time," Fred said, jabbing, as she took up a defensive position back to back with Gunn.

"Remind me to rent next time," Gunn responded as he took a roundhouse swing at the nearest demon. Fred ducked automatically as she felt him shift his weight, so most of the mess that was the demon's head went flying past her. Gunn reversed the crowbar in almost the same movement and came back in the other direction and got another one.

"Maybe they're just jealous," Fred offered, stepping on a flipper-shaped foot and driving efficiently up through what would have been a rib cage. The Tovateir shrieked and flapped its arms. Fred yanked the thing's guts out, pulled it down, and smashed a foot down on its neck. The demon's writhing did the rest of the job for her. *Squish.* "You should have asked if they wanted some popcorn."

It wasn't a pleasure trip to the movies. From the school ID information Fred had gotten from the computers, they'd identified several kids who had been taking lab classes at the school, and Cordelia had picked out several who looked familiar. Lorne, a demon friend, had reported a tip about kids stirring things up in the dimensions from one of his contacts in the demonic underworld of Los Angeles. Another vision sent Fred and Gunn to the theater, where at least one of the kids had worked. But they had arrived too late.

Gunn had broken in, and they found the remains of melted candles everywhere. The floor of the stage before the movie screen was marked up with several half-erased Circles of Power. There was quite a lot of blood, too, and the remains of a letter jacket. It looked like whatever had come through had eaten well. There was nothing alive anywhere, except the roaches in the concession area. Fred wondered how the police would cover up this mess.

They'd been on their way back to the car when they got jumped.

Fred dropped flat beside a Dumpster, wrinkling her nose at the smell. Tovateirs were bad enough, but garbage, too?

Except, well, another Tovateir shambled past her, and she swept its feet out from under it, dancing back from the swiping fingernails. She might not be able to deal with the garbage, but she could always fight demons. Nothing like aerobic exercise to finish up the day.

She heard Gunn cry out, and then curse.

Either the shrieking had temporarily deafened her, or the clicking wasn't as loud anymore. Fred looked up and realized not only was her companion no longer at her back, but that the battle had shifted farther down the alley, where someone else had joined in. She could only see a swirl of shadows against the dim light, but it was enough to tell her that the number of Tovateirs was noticeably less. She looked around for a better weapon, grabbed the lid of a trash can, and ran to rejoin the battle.

She got there just in time to knock down the last of the Tovateirs, preventing a fatal blow. The muttered curse and grunt of recovery was enough to identify their unscheduled support. She rolled out of the way in time to avoid the machete chop that took off the demon's head and then propped herself on her elbows to look up their rescuer.

He was looking pretty good. Too well dressed to be standing in an alley: dark shirt with a high collar, nice slacks. The scarf around his neck had come loose, not quite hiding the shadow that she knew was once a really ugly-looking scar. Fading now, but still . . .

Fred smiled. "Fancy meeting you here, Wesley."

He threw her an inscrutable glance—he specialized in inscrutable looks these days—and finished wiping demon goop off the machete blade. The blade slid into its sheath with a *snick,* and he started to reach out, reflexively, to offer her a hand up. Then his hand froze in mid-gesture, as if he abruptly remembered it wasn't just the two of them, after all.

Gunn. Where was Gunn?

Gunn was sagging against a dented Dumpster, panting, glaring at Wes as if he was just daring him to offer a lady a hand. Men. Honestly. Fred got her own self to her feet and went over to see if Gunn was hurt.

He had a pretty deep cut on the bicep of his right arm, and a couple of scratches on his left shoulder, but nothing too bad.

Fred turned back to Wesley, who had started to walk away, sliding the machete into some kind of sheath, and then shrugging on a coat over that. He must have taken off the coat before he waded into the fight. Nice to know he felt he could take the time. "Wesley."

He paused. Turned his head. Didn't—quite—turn around. Didn't say anything.

"Thanks. We appreciate the help. You saved our butts." She kicked Gunn in the ankle, hard.

He didn't quite smother a yelp, but added grumpily, "Yeah. Good timing."

Wesley said something, kept on walking past the corpses of the demons, already beginning to swarm with rats.

Fred and Gunn looked at each other. Fred's brow furrowed. "Did he really say, 'You're welcome'?"

"Damn, I think he did," Gunn replied. "Devil's gonna wear a sweater tonight."

The not-so-secret ambition of every student at the Watchers Academy, of course, had been to be the Watcher of an Active Slayer. It was what they studied for, what they dreamed of. They had secretly pitied any Watcher whose Slayer-in-Waiting was never Chosen, and they read and studied and argued passionately about the chronicles of those fortunate ones who guided the careers of the Chosen Ones—the Chosen One in every generation. (There were several more than one per generation, of course, but it sounded better that way, and it was traditional, after all. The Watchers were great ones for tradition.)

Wesley Wyndam-Pryce could remember vividly the occasion when a Watcher whose Slayer had been killed had returned to the Academy to submit his chronicle to the Watchers Archives. Wesley's father had told him—quite privately, of course— that they had tried to persuade the man to speak to the students at the Academy about his experiences as a Watcher, but the man had refused. A few months later he had committed suicide. The gossip at the Academy had been frightful, speculating on how he had failed his Slayer.

The chronicles were always sealed to anyone but the Council until after the deaths of the Watchers involved, but he had died so quickly, they'd got to review it very soon after the actual events. Wesley remembered being fascinated by it, thinking he would never have made the choices the Watcher had made.

Little did he know.

The students had studied ancient languages, demonology, occultism, dimensionality, the physics of magick. The best of them could recite the most intricate relationships of seven or eight inhuman, nonhuman, and demonic systems. Wesley had been one of the best of them. ("For his year," his father had said.) He had been Head Boy, top of his class academically, a member of the upper class, and good at sports, too. The kinds of sports the Watchers Academy went for, that is: Japanese and Chinese martial arts, stick and blade fighting. He had kept the rest of the students in line, making sure they knew what an honor it was to carry on the traditions of the Watchers, to guide the Slayers in the battle against the vampires, against evil. He had always known that he would be one of the lucky ones selected to Watch the Chosen.

And so he had been.

"And bloody bugger all good it did," he muttered hoarsely, examining the reflection of the long, weeping cut across his chest in the bathroom mirror. Another shirt ruined. Reaching into the medicine cabinet, he took out an unlabeled jar of dark reddish-blue ointment, opened it, and sniffed it carefully before dipping a couple of fingers into it. Gritting his teeth, he closed his eyes and smeared a liberal amount of the stuff into the cut.

Despite himself, his breath hissed out between his teeth and his head jerked back in involuntary protest as the ointment met the venom from the Tovateir's claws, but he dug into the jar again and again, until the cut was thoroughly coated and the blood no longer dripped across his belly. His hand was shaking slightly when he reached to turn on the hot water to rinse the thick gel away.

He'd have to make up more of the stuff soon, he thought as he placed the lid on the jar and put it away. He held up his hands and watched them dispassionately, forcing the shock reaction to stop. One more like this would use up his supply. He'd do it tomorrow.

Remembering Gunn's arm wound, he knew Gunn was in for a bad night. Perhaps next time he wouldn't be so eager to escort Fred past dark alleys, risking a young woman's life, risking *Fred's* life—

Stop that.

He reached for the gauze and began the awkward process of wrapping it around himself, around his chest and over one shoulder to hold it in place.

Did they have enough of the ointment, over at the Hyperion, to take care of all their cuts? At least Fred was all right—

Part of him asked savagely, *Why should I care whether they have enough of the proper supplies at Angel Investigations?* but the greater part knew why. He cared because they had been his friends, his comrades. They had been like family. When he was a part of Angel Investigations, he had been a part of something important.

Then he had tried to save the life of Angel's son by taking him away from his father, attempting to thwart a prophecy that said "the father will kill the son." He had ended up with his throat slit, and when his friends and coworkers had found him, Angel, raging, had tried to strangle him.

Perhaps Angel no longer hated him, but that wasn't the sort of thing one forgot in a hurry. He wasn't quite able to forgive and forget, not quite yet. It was better now than it had been, but—

He shut off that line of thought. What would be, would be.

He finished tying off the gauze and had started back to the apartment's living room and the cell phone he'd left on the coffee table when the door buzzer sounded.

For a moment he didn't recognize the sound. He couldn't recall the last time anyone had rung the doorbell.

It sounded again.

He stepped to the door and checked the security viewer. A young man stood in the light of the landing, eyes narrowed, staring directly at the camera lens.

Not many would even have known there *was* a camera lens. "Good heavens," Wesley murmured, and then, louder, as he thumbed the intercom switch, he said, "Just a moment, please."

It wouldn't do to greet a visitor half-dressed. He went into the bedroom, found a dark T-shirt, and paused long enough to make sure that the bandage didn't show through it before going back to the door and opening it.

"Yes?" He was aware that he didn't sound particularly warm and welcoming, but he never could seem to generate a friendly facade, and lately it had been even more of a challenge than usual.

The man standing in front of the door turned back from an inspection of the street in front of the apartment. He had his hands thrust deep into his jacket pockets, and didn't withdraw them. He looked like a college student, as if he'd hit his mid-twenties and simply stopped aging. He was lean rather than slender, not too tall, with clear, sharp hazel-brown eyes that were older and wearier than the rest of him, a shock of brown hair, a nose rather too large for his face. When he looked up at Wesley, he didn't smile, but he was relaxed, open,

43

friendly. And there was just a hint of a highborn drawl in his voice. "Wyndam-Pryce? It's O'Flaherty. Adrian O'Flaherty. You remember me?"

As if he could forget.

The sixth form was nearing Final Examinations, and a mandated year of freedom before they would make the Decision whether to swear the Oath or abandon the Council's work completely. The year was supposed to allow the class time to think about the responsibility they'd be taking on, the burdens of the Watchers Oath.

Publicly, of course, every member of every class spoke openly of taking the Oath; no one wanted to show a yellow streak. And excitement was at a fever pitch, because at night, after lights were out, whispers ran from one end of the dormitories to the other about what lay on the other side of the swearing-in. Typically, he thought, they were focused upon taking the Oath and not upon the necessary steps they would have to take to get there. He, at least, had paid attention, and he knew that a good proportion of every class never even got through exams, much less got sworn in. It was a waste of time to speculate, time that could be better spent studying.

Yet no matter how late the Head Boy patrolled the hallways, no matter how exhausting the physical training was, even if he deliberately rapped on the doors as he went he could hear the voices, as if the examinations could be taken for granted. They spent no time studying at all.

"They say the Council comes in white robes and summons up a demon—"

"No, it's three demons—"

"You have to cut your arm and give them blood to drink—"

"Ah, that's bollocks, you've never seen old Ginnivray with a scar on his arm."

"It's a magickal scar, that's why. It only shows up when there's black magick about—"

"Lights out! Quiet in there!"

Giggles, a few of them still high-pitched. And the voices would stop for a moment or two and then they'd start up again.

The wildest rumors always came from the same source. Naturally.

"I hear they take the Head Girl and test her to see if she's a Slayer-in-Waiting, and if she isn't, they'll do a ritual sacrifice."

And that hated voice that he pretended not to hear, drawling: "Sure they won't do the Head Boy instead?"

A protest. Stephens, right out of the Basics: "Ritual sacrifices have to be virgins, don't they?"

"Well, I hear that doesn't stop Pryce from qualifying!"

More giggles.

And he couldn't bring himself to tell them to be quiet again. He moved on down the hall, as silently as he could, back to his own, private room, privilege of being Head Boy, and buried himself in the consolation of making sure that he, at least, was perfectly prepared. He didn't require the camaraderie of those cretins. He could absorb himself in the minutiae of the arcane instead, and build up walls of thick, comforting volumes, a veritable fortress of knowledge not one of them could challenge. He might not be well liked, but he was better organized for Examinations than any of them. He was sure of it.

And the next day, in History and Ritual, he pretended his glasses were smudged, so that he didn't have to look O'Flaherty in the eye. The bastard knew he'd still been standing outside the door the night before, he was sure of it. He'd said all that knowing that Wesley could hear him.

The little shite grinned at him and flung his books onto the desk, sprawled across the aisle to tug on Lancaster's sleeve and whisper something in his ear, and the two of them glanced back at him and laughed. He glared back, noting their uncombed hair, unpressed trousers. Lancaster was missing a button on his blazer. Had they no pride? He knew that O'Flaherty was a legacy admission to the Academy, since his father was important in the Library—it was said that Gabriel O'Flaherty

*would even be the head of the Library next year;
and how a man like that could have sired a son
with so little respect for books and scrolls as that
young pup was beyond Wesley Wyndam-Pryce's
comprehension—but how the devil did Lancaster
manage to stay in? Wesley himself had given him a
dozen demerits within the last month alone.*

But he couldn't think, None of them have any
class, *because that reminded him too sharply of his
own father's reaction when he had announced at
dinner one evening that he had been made Head
Boy:* "They must not have many to choose from,
then." *And he hadn't even bothered to look at the
letter of announcement.*

He had the accent of home. Of England, despite
the very Irish name. He'd been able to sound as
English as the Queen Mum or as Irish as Paddy's
pig if he chose, Wesley remembered. Oh, he
remembered Adrian O'Flaherty. The Fearsome
O'Flaherty. He didn't look very fearsome, did he,
standing on one's doorstep at nearly midnight. But
he never had, had he? Unless you looked at his
eyes. No matter how young he looked, those eyes
gave him away. They'd seen too much.

"You do remember me?"

Wesley shrugged away the memories. "Yes, of
course."

"Aren't you going to ask me in?" The hated

drawl was gone, and now the accent was a pleasant BBC British, and there was a glint of laughter in the hazel-brown eyes.

Wesley smiled thinly, reached out of the other man's line of sight to an aspergillum resting conveniently within reach, and dashed a spray of holy water across O'Flaherty's face.

Startled, O'Flaherty blinked and shook his head at the sudden splash; what he did *not* do was burst into flames or scream in agony.

Instead, he laughed, recognizing the greeting for what it was.

"Certainly," Wesley said. "Please, come in. It's been, what? A dozen years?"

"Oh, at least that," O'Flaherty responded, wiping a trickle of consecrated water off his cheek as he stepped across the threshold. "I should have called first, but I was in the neighborhood and thought I'd look you up."

"Really? How interesting. I was just about to step out, I'm afraid—but let me instead make a call. Sit down. I'll fix you a drink." A tangle of conflicting impulses had Wesley momentarily nonplussed. He resolved at least one by finding a bottle of decent English ale and pouring his unexpected guest a glass.

"Do you often find vampires on your doorstep?" O'Flaherty asked, accepting the drink. He hadn't taken advantage of the invitation to sit down. He was wandering around the living room, looking at things. It made Wesley uneasy.

"More often than you'd think. Sit down. Please."

The other man's head turned sharply at his tone, and then he smiled and raised his glass as if in a toast. He took a seat on the battered leather couch, leaning back into the cushion as if it were the most comfortable resting place he'd found in a long while. He sipped at the ale, rolling the liquid around his tongue as one would a fine wine, before he swallowed it. "You said you had a call to make, Pryce? Don't let me keep you. I'm absolutely marvelous here."

He looked as if nothing short of Armageddon would move him. But he was O'Flaherty, and Wesley remembered better than that. Picking up the cell phone, Wes retreated to the kitchen, keeping an eye on the recumbent man through the open doorway, and called Angel Investigations.

"Cordelia? Have Fred and Gunn got back yet? Good. Do you have enough d'nuluath ointment on hand for him? D'nuluath ointment. D'nuluath . . . Let me talk to Lorne—he's not there. All ri—" His voice flattened suddenly. "Angel."

The man on the couch could tell the difference in his voice, even if he couldn't distinguish the words. O'Flaherty could probably read his body language, too, Wesley thought—he'd drawn himself up defensively just at the sound of Angel's voice. Not that Wesley was afraid of him. Just that things were still . . . not easy . . . between them.

"I was calling to make sure you had sufficient d'nuluath ointment on hand for Gunn's injuries," he said, keeping his voice as professional and formal as he could. It was just as well that he hadn't gone over there, anyway.

The response on the other end of the line wasn't what he'd expected. It was far more cordial, almost coaxing. "D'nuluath? That's the purple stuff, right? Stings like hell? We've got enough for tonight, but I was going to ask you if you'd show Cordy how to make the stuff up. We're going to run out."

"You were *what*?" he could hear Cordelia yelp in the background. "I don't cook or do ointments!"

"And besides," Angel plowed on, undeterred, "there's something else I'd like you to do, if you've got time. If you don't mind."

A pause, which stretched out longer and longer while Angel waited for him to ask what it was he wanted, and Wesley considered the olive branch being offered in the request. O'Flaherty arched an eyebrow and then looked away, sipping once more at his drink in studied, pointed indifference.

Wesley found himself rubbing, reflexively, at the phantom itch in the scar on his neck.

O'Flaherty had carefully not noticed that, either. As if it didn't exist.

"Certainly," Wesley said abruptly. "What is it?"

If vampires could breathe, the sound he heard might have been a tiny sigh of relief. "Great. This is right up your alley. There's an auction of rare books day after tomorrow—"

"The Gilman collection?" He'd been hearing about it for weeks. The occult world was abuzz with the news that the arcane sale of the century was going to be conducted right there in Los Angeles. The auctioneers, Melchior's, hadn't had to advertise; all they'd had to do was drop a few hints, and everyone wanted to be on the invitation-only bidders' list.

Now O'Flaherty was definitely eavesdropping, making no attempt to hide it.

"Yes. They're having it in the garden of the Egan mansion, in the middle of the afternoon." Wesley could hear the vampire's frustration. If Angel tried to attend a sunlit auction, he'd burst into flames. "I'd appreciate it if you'd go and see who else is there and what they're bidding on. I want to know if anybody is trying to collect a pattern of artifacts or grimoires. If so, we'll try to predict this team of wizard wanna-bes' next move."

"Grasping at straws, don't you think?"

"This is the biggest collection to come on the market in years. It's not just Gilman's; a bunch of the occult stores up and down the coast have piggybacked on it as well. If they show up any-where, they'll show up there. And you're the best qualified person I know to spot those connections. You've got the training, the experience."

Madame Shearer came in, and Wesley snapped to his feet, a good half-second before the rest of the class had even noticed the presence of their professor. He sometimes thought they simply waited for him to stand before it even dawned on him that a professor had entered a classroom. Let him be the lookout while they continued their juvenile chatter. How typical.

Madame Shearer was a neat, birdlike woman of indeterminate age, with elegantly coiffed hair and exquisite taste in jewelry—rose quartz, Wesley had noticed, and diamonds, an interesting combination. Diamonds, he could understand; they were her birthstone, and were powerful talismans for repelling demons and preventing evil. But rose quartz? Quartz was for storing energy, for healing; the pale pink variety was used in fertility spells! And Madame Shearer was not a motherly sort of woman.

She was never seen without a pashmina about her shoulders—today's was peacock blue, shot with green and gold thread, shimmering in the light from the tall, narrow classroom windows.

She observed her class as much as taught it, he thought, and he tried hard to be worthy of her observation, feeling the weight of her thoughtful gray gaze as if it were one of the rapiers in the

Fencing class, ready to flick blood if he was not paying proper attention.

Today, however, she seemed to look inward rather than outward. She strode briskly to the podium at the head of the classroom and grasped the slanted edges with both hands as she looked over the faces of teenage boys and girls who made up the sixth form, and they stared back at her, slightly bewildered.

"Ladies and gentlemen." This was one of the things Wesley most appreciated about the Academy; once one had passed the first form, one was always addressed in the most formal terms. Let barbarians like O'Flaherty make fun of it if they would; it made him feel almost—well, not equal of course, one couldn't consider oneself an equal to a fully sworn Watcher until one had taken the Oath oneself. But potentially an equal.

Madame Shearer paused, cleared her throat, and began again. "Ladies and gentlemen. As you are aware, the time is fast approaching when each of you will be asked to make some very serious decisions about the course your life will take. It is not an exaggeration to say that these decisions will shape not only your future, but possibly the future of the entire human race. At the very least, lives will rest upon your willingness to take up a burden for which we have done our best to prepare you."

• • •

Wesley considered, then looked over at his visitor. "Why don't I come over tomorrow to help with that ointment," he said to the vampire, "and we can discuss the details."

"Great. We'll see you then."

Wesley disconnected and set the phone down, and turned to fix a drink of his own before joining the other man in the living room.

O'Flaherty gestured to the glass in Wesley's hand. "On the wagon, then?"

"I beg your pardon?"

"It's good of you to save the good stuff for your guests, but you're drinking ginger ale?"

Wesley smiled thinly. "Out of the habit." He took a long swallow and asked, "So, Adrian O'Flaherty, what brings you to the neighborhood? Not that I'm not glad to see that someone else escaped the—disaster."

O'Flaherty nodded, looking into the half-inch of dark brown liquid remaining in his glass. He raised it to his lips, swallowing it all down.

Wesley waited him out, getting up to refill the glass held out to him and going back to the easy chair across the coffee table from the couch.

"You were there?" he asked, as if asking, *You were there at the university . . . at the boat show . . . at the street fair?* Not as if he was asking, *You were there at the explosion that wiped out the Watchers Headquarters and Council and killed untold dozens of our friends, teachers, mentors, colleagues?*

"Yes, actually. It was rather . . ." He looked at the glass in his hand as if surprised to see it full again, and put it down on the coffee table. "So. Did I hear you mention the Gilman collection?"

Wesley made a noncommittal noise.

"That's why I'm in town, in fact. To attend that auction. See if there's anything interesting." He looked up and offered that engaging, charming smile that Wesley the Head Boy had learned to mistrust to his very bones. "After all, it's all we know to do, isn't it? Chase the demons. Thought I'd call on you and see what the territory was like. You've been here a while, I'd heard."

And maybe see another former Watcher and not feel so alone in the world. Wesley could understand that. "So are you planning on staying in L.A., then?"

He laughed. "I'm not the kind to settle. A vampire here, a demon there, and the broad highway for me. You stay in one place, you run out of surprises. You know that."

A flicker of mischief, an opportunity to pay back, perhaps, a few of the practical jokes a younger O'Flaherty had played on a far too priggish Head Boy, lit up in Wesley Wyndam-Pryce. "So you're looking for surprises, then?"

O'Flaherty shrugged. The slug of liquor was

beginning to have a decided effect.

"I may have one for you," Wesley suggested gently. "Perhaps you'd like to come with me tomorrow and meet the staff at . . . where I . . . used to work."

CHAPTER FOUR

"I don't *do* Martha Stewart," Cordelia repeated. "I do fashion. Fashion on a budget, true, but still, not curtains. Not cute table settings. And definitely not ointments."

Angel shrugged. Cordy wasn't *that* annoyed about it. She wasn't above throwing things when she got really angry.

Fred came down the stairs from the mezzanine to the main lobby.

"How's Gunn?" Cordy asked, switching focus and mood so fast, it would have given whiplash to anyone not used to her special gift for it.

Fred was looking even paler than usual. "He's asleep," she said. "It was pretty Tarantino." She was carrying a purple-stained towel, using it to dry her hands, and made a face as she scrubbed at the stains. "How long will it take to heal with that stuff?"

"He'll be on his feet tomorrow, but not demon-hunter extraordinare for the next few days. Probably ought to avoid trouble." Angel was sitting on a stool by what had once been the check-in desk, tapping a pencil against the glossy wood.

"So? What?" Cordy had swung her attention back to him again.

Angel shook his head. "I'm not sure what. I wish Lorne had more information about those kids. I want more to go on than just—*vagueness.*"

"Vague is good," Fred and Cordelia said, at almost the same time, and looked at each other, sharing an embarrassed grin.

"It is," Cordelia went on. "Vague means nobody we know is eating anybody. And I'm all for nobody getting eaten."

"No, vague means we can't pin down the problem," Angel muttered. "I don't like it."

"Maybe it isn't really a problem," Fred offered. "Lorne could have been wrong." Off the looks she got in response, she backtracked. "Or the kids could have changed their mind."

"Or not," Angel muttered.

"Probably not," Cordy agreed. "That would be too easy. And when did things ever get easy?" She snorted. "The easy, we do immediately. The impossible, we send out for pizza and think about for a while. Who wants pepperoni?"

• • •

"Artie, why don't you quit now and go to bed? You can finish packing up everything from the back room tomorrow."

"Uh, yeah." Artie stood in the mess of papers and books and bills and scraps of stained paper bags and shoved his glasses up on the bridge of his nose, looking around desperately. They all looked alike, the books back here, piled on the old desk and the shelves against the back wall and the floor and even on the old radiator—the covers all dull grayish green and greenish gray and brownish grayish greenish, spines separated or missing entirely, pages coming loose. The place smelled of mildew and old coffee and paper and dust.

His uncle Tobey had important stuff, he was nearly sure of it. He and his mom had come on visits a few times after his father's death, and enough people had come to the store when he was there, people who kept quiet about who they were and paid cash, people who told the old man about books they wanted and where they could be reached. And sometimes Uncle Tobey called them and they came back all eager. Mom said her brother-in-law was a failure, but Artie didn't think so. He'd even seen one guy crying the day Uncle Tobey handed him a little funny-sized book— he kept touching it, running his hands over it, and he cried, and he didn't even open it to look at it, just stared down at the cover and turned it over and over and kept thanking Uncle Tobey. Weird.

So there was important stuff here somewhere, but how the heck was he supposed to be able to tell what it was?

Unless this was just the junk stuff. After Uncle Tobey had vanished and everybody had finally accepted he wasn't gonna come back, Mom had started selling most of the front store stock. Man, it was like, like piranhas on a cow or something, the way everything disappeared, in only three days. He and Mom both figured the stuff back here was just crap and they were gonna shovel it in a Dumpster.

But then they'd got this letter about the auction. And Mom figured she'd probably priced stuff in the store too low, the way it had all disappeared. So what the hell. She was really ticked off about it because it all really belonged to her anyway. Uncle Tobey had kept borrowing money from her to buy stuff and nobody ever could find out what the heck he was borrowing it for. There wasn't anything here that *looked* valuable.

But if there *was* something important in here, couldn't he find it and sell it himself? Couldn't he find just *one* thing to sell for himself? That guy who cried, he might want one of these books.

If he could just find a Rolodex or something. It was too much to expect the old man to have had a computer, but he had to have had addresses for his customers somewhere in here!

"Artie! It's late! I want to get these boxes loaded up in the van tonight!"

He sighed, and kicked at one of the books he'd shoved off its stack in his frustration. Stupid thing wasn't even in English. How could it be worth anything?

"Okay, Mom." They were staying in Uncle Tobey's deserted apartment over the store until the place was cleared out. Artie pushed at another stack of books, dumped them into a box, and clumped out of his late uncle's office, slamming the door behind him in frustration.

Behind him, the pages of the books still on the floor whispered in the movement of the air.

Gunn woke the next morning feeling nauseated, sore, and angry, in no particular order. He knew it was morning because light poured across his bed from the window in the eastern wall, the window that never had any curtains or shades because he thought it was always good to know when the sun was up. He could smell coffee, too, and pancakes, the odors of breakfast coming from somewhere downstairs. Unfortunately, that intersected with "nausea," which sent him staggering to the bathroom, and that triggered "sore," and that didn't help "angry" at all.

So when Fred knocked on the door—a diffident knock designed to not disturb a resting invalid—his response was less than encouraging.

"*What?*"

Either his roar of rage needed work, or Fred had a lot more spine than she used to. Probably both, he admitted to himself as he sagged against the frame of the bathroom door, panting. Fred took the roar as permission to enter, sighed, and steered him back to the bed.

"I'm not going to lie down, dammit. I'm on my feet, I'm gonna stay that way."

"You need to rest, Charles."

"I need to be on my feet. I'm not bleeding. Look." The bandages on his arm were stained purple, not red. "It's that damn jelly you put on me that made me throw up. I'm okay now."

Fred's lips tightened, and she avoided his gaze as she cut away the bandage and examined the wound the Tovateir's claws had carved in the heavy muscles of Gunn's upper arm. The d'nuluath had crusted over the wound. "Hold your arm still," she ordered, and went into the bathroom.

Gunn sat on the edge of the bed, arm in the air, feeling foolish. Looking down at himself, he felt even more foolish as he realized that in the middle of holding him down to get the stuff in his arm the night before—and he did remember that part, it was hard not to remember screaming that loud—somebody had undressed him and then put a pair of clean boxers on him.

Well, maybe not in the middle. Maybe more

toward the end. Because he didn't remember about the boxers, and he was absolutely sure he would have remembered *that* if he'd been in any shape to at all.

Fred came out with a wet washcloth and swabbed away some of the excess dried gel, pressing lightly at the edges of the wound, checking for infection. It was clean, already starting to knit, but that didn't mean it didn't hurt. Gunn was focusing hard on his Zen breathing, in and out, slow and calm, by the time she had finished wrapping it up again.

When she started to bind his arm to his chest, he objected. "I need to be able to move."

"You need to be able to heal." They stared at each other for a full thirty seconds, and he finally gave in. Okay, he'd play it her way for *one* day. He could use the practice using his other arm, anyway.

"Let me get my pants on first, at least."

By the time they had come down the stairs there was a light film of sweat across his brow, and he was glad the staircase had a railing to lean on. Fred went ahead of him. It wasn't as if she could break his fall or anything, but he suspected that that was what she had in mind, so he took it slow and easy. Hey, it made for a grand entrance, right?

"Your scrambled eggs are getting cold," Cordy informed him as he got to the lobby. She and Lorne had set up a buffet against a far wall, and he could now smell eggs and bacon as well as coffee and pancakes. The nausea had vanished; he was starving. If a horse had been tethered by the plates, it would be in serious trouble.

"Good morning! If it isn't our wounded hero!" Lorne caroled. Lorne was one of the more unusual friends Angel Investigations had cultivated. He was a demon addicted to swing and jazz, and he ran his own nightclub, Caritas, and hung out a lot at the Hyperion Hotel, where the rest of them made their headquarters. "Welcome back to the land of the—well, welcome back! Sit yourself down, babycakes. I don't normally do the waitstaff thing, but I can make an exception, today only, priced as marked. . . ."

"What's he talking about?" Gunn growled, reaching for coffee.

"Feeding you. Sit down," Cordy said, taking over from an obviously relieved Fred. Gunn allowed himself to be maneuvered to an overstuffed red velvet chair, as long as he was still facing both the front door and the buffet. Lorne heaped a plate with still-steaming eggs, bacon, a stack of pancakes, and a dollop of syrup for good measure, scooped up silverware, whipped a napkin across his arm, and presented it all to Gunn with an elaborate bow.

"Coffee," Gunn mumbled through a mouthful of food.

"The man has no appreciation for presentation. None," Lorne complained.

Cordy set a mug of coffee on the table in front of the walking wounded. "Ignore him," she said. It wasn't clear who she was advising to ignore whom, so each was free to assume she was addressing him, and give a vindicated mutter.

"How's the arm?"

Gunn looked up to see Angel coming out of the back office, the combination library/workroom/ weapons storage/research center. Gunn's mouth was full, so he settled for nodding and waving his fork in an indeterminate *I'm okay* gesture. Angel nodded and kept going, passing the buffet table without so much as a flare of the nostrils. That was interesting, Gunn thought; his hunger was sufficiently sated that he could pause and observe such minor details. Naturally Angel wouldn't show any interest in the food as food, but normally he'd at least react to the rich smells. And if they were rich and enticing to mere human senses—

Well, he'd find out soon enough what was bothering the founder of Angel Investigations. He finished his meal and sat back, sipping at his coffee with a sigh of contentment. None of these ladylike cups for him. He wanted a mug big enough to get him through a morning. One he could swim in, if the impulse struck him.

Angel gave him a quick smile and stopped to talk to Cordy; the two of them went back into the office together. Lorne and Fred had taken plates to the other end of the lobby and were deep in discussion about something or other, probably extra-dimensional.

As a result, he was the only one who happened to be looking at the front door when it opened and Wesley Wyndam-Pryce brought Adrian O'Flaherty to Angel Investigations.

Wes didn't see him right away, and that was fine with Gunn.

"Hello? Is anyone here?"

Gunn sat unmoving, watching the tall, lean, dark-haired figure, wondering who his new buddy was. Young, wiry little guy, nondescript brown hair, standing there with his hands shoved in his pockets, looking around at everything. Those sharp hazel-brown eyes didn't miss much—he spotted Gunn sitting there at the same time Wes did, maybe even an instant before. Didn't say anything; waited to see what the lay of the land was.

Maybe he wasn't as young as he looked.

Huh, thought Gunn. *Doesn't act like a new client. No "my-god-I've-seen-a-monster" hysterics. Pretty calm and self-possessed, in fact. So what have we got here, Wesley my man?*

The guy followed Wes. Wes had the sense to stop just far enough back so he wasn't looming over a man sitting down. So did his friend.

"Charles. Good to see you up and about. Suffering no lasting effects from our unfortunate encounter, I trust?"

That was Wes. Never use one word when a dozen would do. "Yeah, I'm good." He set down the mug. "Who's your friend?"

Wes smiled thinly, and a little alarm started going off in the back of Gunn's mind. That wasn't a *my friend* kind of smile, not when Wesley smiled it. "This is a former colleague of mine. Charles Gunn, may I present Adrian O'Flaherty?"

O'Flaherty stepped forward and offered his left hand. "Nice to meet you."

Gunn shook it awkwardly, thinking, *Smooth dude. Most people would have offered their right hand and gone all flustered when they saw my arm all tied up.* This guy had seen and compensated automatically. Another Brit, too. As if they needed another one.

"O'Flaherty, is it?" Angel and Cordelia had come out of the back office again at the sound of voices. The name sounded different when Angel said it. Less Brit, more green-hills-and-Clancy-Brotherish. Angel came across the lobby toward them and stopped only ten feet or so away from the newcomers.

Wesley turned to him to make the introductions, giving Gunn an excellent view of O'Flaherty's face as he turned, just as Wesley said, "And this, of course, is Angel, for whom Angel Investigations is named."

CHAPTER FIVE

"Yeah," Emilio said. "I can do this. I can do a lot more, too." He grinned at Victoria and the four others sitting around the backyard with him. "I can call things you wouldn't believe. It's all right here."

His hand slapped down on the pile of books.

"He can, for sure," Victoria confirmed. Her voice was thin, but she was quick to back him up. She hadn't seen what had happened to Tim Markowitz, but she'd heard it as she'd run for her life. She wasn't going to tell the others that Emilio had been right behind her. Emilio said he'd had it under control. And he must have, because the thing didn't follow them.

Now Emilio wanted to impress more of the kids, and she had to back him up. She didn't want to think what would happen if she didn't.

"Show me," one of the others said, still skeptical.

"Okay," Emilio responded, "I will. Not here,

though. You want to see something big, we're going to need some space. And I know where, too." He'd taken his sister to enough lessons, after all.

"Artie, you follow that man there while I get the rest of these boxes ready." Mrs. Cawber was staring into the back of the van, shaking her head. Honestly, it was a good thing the guy was only a guard. If the auction people could see this mess, they'd throw them right out. This was a really nice place.

"Maaaaaa—" Artie sounded a lot like a sheep when he whined.

The security man looked at Artie as if he shared the same thought—and was a wolf wondering if wool was on the Atkins diet. With an effort, he shifted his attention away from the boy and back to the contents of the van. "Four boxes, right? Miscellaneous books? That's it?"

Mrs. Cawber stiffened. He didn't have to sneer like that. "That's what we agreed to bring. We can take them in—"

"Only one of you can come in. The boy can bring them. The full amount we agreed upon is right here." He held out a manila envelope.

Mrs. Cawber took the envelope and counted its contents, making sure the man could watch her do it. She didn't trust him, either, not one bit.

Oblivious, Artie stood with a box in his arms, shifting his weight from one foot to the other.

"Ma, I gotta *go*," he said finally.

"Why don't you come with me," the guard said, obviously tired of waiting, "and I'll show you where to put the box and where the bathroom is. Then you can come back and get the rest. You"—he said directly to Mrs. Cawber—"will stay here. There's someone on duty inside."

"Yeah, okay."

Mrs. Cawber barely glanced after them. The people they hired these days! She was sure the man had had to go through all kinds of checks before he could work at a place like this—she was surprised they even let them in the door without doing a full background investigation—but he didn't have to be *that* rude. As if she was going to steal something. Honestly.

She shook her head again and started putting books in the boxes, spines up, sorting them by size and color. It didn't really matter. Some of them didn't even have spines. Most of them were dingy brown. But at least she could make them look neater. Her brother-in-law would have liked that.

Artie was back in a few minutes, hands empty, looking considerably refreshed. "Hey Ma, this place is, like, Baghdad! They must be *really* rich here. I think the faucets in the bathroom are real gold!"

"That's just brass, Artie. It looks like gold."

"I seen brass in the Lowe's, Ma, and this don't look like that."

"Don't argue. Here, take this." She shoved another cardboard box into his arms and climbed into the back of the van to wrestle another one forward. "You made a mess of this, you know what. You didn't have to do that. Every time I ask you to do something, I end up having to do it myself. Every single time."

"Oh, Ma." There he went again, sounding like a sheep. "They said I could stay to help, after."

"Like you could do anything here."

"They said!"

Actually, she thought, that wouldn't be too bad. She could go by Maisie's, go to the bank, maybe even pay a couple of bills with the deposit money, and she wouldn't have to listen to him complaining every step of the way. "All right, all right. But get this done first. I'll pick you up in about three hours."

She could hear him shuffling away, his feet dragging on the gravel. Sulking again, probably. He was always sulking.

She got the last two boxes organized and had them sitting beside the van by the door. She was waiting for Artie to come back out to get them, when her cell phone rang.

"Maisie? Hi, hon—oh my gosh, is it that time

already? I was just dropping off some things of Tobey's. . . . Oh. Well, I guess I could leave now, if you need me right away—sure, hon, it's no trouble, I can do that." She glanced over at the door, at the boxes.

Artie knew she'd be back to pick him up. She looked at her watch. "Okay, hon, I'll be right there. Don't try to do too much, now."

She got into the van and drove away, leaving the boxes beside the door.

The security guard was at the door only moments later, watching the van trundle down the driveway to the gate. *Humans,* he thought. First the kid drops a whole box of books on the ground by the garden tables, then the two of them drive off. He should never have paid her in advance. He'd already had to stack the damned grimoires, and now they left the rest of them here for him to haul inside. So help him Belial, he swore, if he ever saw that woman again, he *would* have her and her kid for lunch. . . .

Shock.

That was the only word for it.

A former colleague—another Watcher. Of course. Another Watcher who would have been thoroughly familiar with the terrible history of the vampire Angelus, and who certainly wouldn't have expected to be introduced to him in the middle of a bright, sunny Los Angeles morning by a fellow Watcher, even a fellow former Watcher. Gunn looked at Wes's face and saw nothing there but the civilized, polite expression of a gentleman introducing one acquaintance to another, and thought, *I don't know what this dude ever did to you, Wes, but I think you just paid him back big-time, and you know it too, don't you? Laughing fit to bust a gut inside, aren't you?*

And Angel, who could smell fear on a human a hundred feet away, simply stood there, as nonthreatening as a vampire possibly could be, and waited to see if O'Flaherty was going to go for a stake or not. Waited to see if he'd heard about Angel as well as Angelus, and if it would make the slightest difference when confronted with the reality of the demon who had slaughtered thousands of people over hundreds of years.

O'Flaherty was chalky pale, and he did sway back an inch or so to get his balance. He stared at Angel as if he couldn't believe what he was seeing. But that was it. Looking at Wes, Gunn could tell that Wes didn't really expect anything different. He'd scared the crap out of the guy, but so far, nobody'd done anything to be horribly embarrassed for.

"O'Fladdery? said Cordelia, breaking the silence that was stretching out way too long. "That's an Irish name, isn't it? We used to have an Irish guy here." She faltered for a moment. "His name was Doyle." She stepped between Angel and the visitor to break the sight line and take his hand—and incidentally reassure him that she had a pulse.

The guy took a deep breath and coughed. "O'Flaherty, actually. Adrian O'Flaherty. Wesley and I were at school together. At the *Watchers Academy*." He said the last two words with ice directed as much at Wesley as at Angel.

"Oh, we know all about that," Cordelia said briskly, "but we've decided not to hold it against him."

"Any friend of Wesley's," Angel said. Gunn noticed that Angel didn't finish the sentence. Wesley noticed it too. O'Flaherty was apparently still recovering from the shock.

"I'm, er . . . it's very, ah, interesting to meet you," he said. "One had heard, of course, but, ah . . ." The words trailed off. Taking another deep breath, he squared his shoulders and held out his hand—his right hand, this time.

He had guts, that was for sure.

Without hesitation, Angel took it. "Glad to meet you. What brings you to town?" He let the hand go again and turned to the buffet table, saying, "You'll think we're terrible hosts. Can we get you some coffee?"

It allowed the man just a moment, a moment in which to look down at his right hand, the hand that had just shaken the hand of a vampire, flex it open and closed, and reassure himself that it was really still there. Look up again at the back turned to him, exposed, vulnerable if you were stupid enough to really think Angelus was going to give anybody that kind of opening, but there it was, Angel, pouring coffee, hospitable, welcoming. Just as if there wasn't any history to even forget about.

Wes was smiling to himself again, a little bit different smile this time, as if he'd just found out he was right about something all along. Something, or someone.

Inadequate! *Wesley thought indignantly.* Six years of intensive physical and mental training could hardly be called inadequate! Why, the language instruction alone, in ancient Egyptian, Sumerian, two dialects of Chinese, Hindustani, as well as the pathetically pedestrian Latin and Greek, set their education apart. Of course the Academy provided the more mundane subjects and O levels and A levels, an excellent preparation for any university anywhere. And no other private school anywhere provided the additional, *specialized* education one found here.

The rest of the class didn't seem to share his indignation. They simply glanced at one another, eyebrows raised. O'Flaherty even rolled his eyes.

"You are very young," Madame Shearer said,

75

and Wesley knew she had seen the insolent expression. "Some things can be learned, unfortunately, only through experience.

"You all know, of course, that only one Slayer is called out of all the potential Slayers; and that a Slayer is called only when her predecessor is dead. Killed." *The teacher's voice was harsh, suddenly.*

The girls in the class paled.

"This also means that, by tradition, only one Watcher at any given time is the Active Watcher, the Watcher who is assigned to the current Slayer. We cannot know who that Watcher will be, because we do not know which potential Slayer will be called. So any individual who is assigned field duty by the Council is considered to be a potential Active Watcher, and field duty is the highest honor, the most important work we do. A Watcher remains the Active Watcher, of course, only so long as the Slayer remains . . . alive."

The class was very still now.

"You have spent six years honing your physical and mental abilities here at the Academy in order to train and prepare potential Slayers. Today, under controlled conditions, for the first time, you will assist a Watcher with years of experience in the field; and you will confront our enemy face-to-face."

And Angel, for his part, held out a cup and saucer to the stranger and waited to see what he would do, and wondered what the hell Wesley was thinking of. *From the fury of the ferocious O'Flahertys, Good Lord deliver us.* It had been a byword in the Ireland of his youth, three hundred or so years ago. This sprig of the O'Flaherty family tree certainly had the cool nerve and self-possession the clan had been noted for. Angel had not missed the way the man moved, or the intent, knowing intelligence in his eyes. He wondered if this Adrian also had the recklessness and violent streak the clan had also been noted for. "Cream? Sugar?"

"Black, thank you," O'Flaherty said steadily, and looked around for a place to sit. He chose a place next to Gunn and sipped at the coffee and nodded. "Thank you."

Of them all, Angel supposed, he was the only one who could hear the tiny chatter of the cup against the saucer when O'Flaherty put it down. "You're welcome," he said. "Any friend of Wesley's," he repeated. *Is what?* he thought. *A friend of mine? Not necessarily!*

O'Flaherty's lips twisted with amusement as he glanced up at the vampire. "I'm not sure that Wes and I are friends, exactly, but it will do for now."

Wes laughed, but there was amusement in it, the joke acknowledged. "The Ferocious O'Flaherty and I were rather at odds now and then, back in the day. He had a tendency to be rather unorthodox, back at the Watchers Academy."

"And you had a tendency to be rather a prig." Said with a bit of a snap as well as a smile, that. "But you seem to have developed quite the sense of humor in the meantime."

Wes might be amused at the results of his little joke, Angel thought, but here was a man who remembered a slight. Wes would do well to remember it. O'Flaherty looked up at him almost challengingly. "So, then. One had heard rumors, but—"

"Wesley! You came!"

Oh, this *is going to be good,* Angel thought, and gave a mental wince.

Lorne swept around the conversation group, Fred in tow, without immediately noticing the addition to their gathering. It was probably a *very* good thing that O'Flaherty had already put the coffee cup down; even a Watcher didn't often run into a green-skinned, red-eyed, horned demon in a blue satin suit advancing with arms spread wide in demonic greeting.

The man definitely had excellent cardiac health. His eyes widened, but he didn't move.

When Fred caught sight of him and said, "Oh! We have a visitor! Hello," O'Flaherty couldn't be blamed for looking at her, for just an instant, as if he expected her, too, to sprout fangs, wings, or something just not in the human line. Angel suspected that Wesley didn't have the heart to tell him that the only thing Fred usually produced in the nonhuman line was a sinister tendency to get involved with thick books about algebra and inter-dimensional mathematics, because being a fellow Watcher—former Watcher, now—the guy probably had the same tendency. And, besides, he didn't look like he was much for listening just now.

"Oopsie," Lorne said. "Am I scaring off a paying customer? Pardon my blushes. They just make me greener, sweetie, I can't help it."

"Adrian, this is Lorne, and this is Fred Burkle," Cordelia said, stepping in fast. "Lorne, Fred, this is Adrian O'Flaherty, a friend of Wesley's."

O'Flaherty actually made it to his feet. Fred held out her hand, and after only the slightest hesitation he took it and bowed slightly while shaking it. Then he took a breath and held out his hand to Lorne, too. "An Extosh demon, I believe?" he said. "I don't think I've ever heard of one who's taken to local tailoring before."

Lorne grinned. "Oh, not Extosh. I'm an immigrant from Pylea. They kicked me out of the home dimension. I figure I'll get my green card any day now. Not that I need one, cupcake, I'm the right color already."

O'Flaherty laughed and sat down again.

Angel shot a look at Gunn, who was watching with barely concealed mirth, and they traded raised eyebrows. Snaps to the visitor. Not only excellent equilibrium, but a sense of humor too.

"So what brings you to Los Angeles?" Angel asked, before anyone else could grab the conversation. The others had filled plates or gotten themselves coffee from the buffet and had seated themselves as well; he was the only one with empty hands. Probably wouldn't be a good idea to treat himself to a shot of goat's blood just now. He didn't want to get into a discussion of his dietary habits; he wanted to know what brought a former Watcher into his territory.

O'Flaherty took a deep breath and stared into the depths of the coffee cup as if he could read fortunes in the dregs there, and then looked up. "I'm wandering," he said, and his voice was as bleak as any human's Angel had ever heard. "We're only trained for the one thing, you know." He met Angel's gaze, and the ghost of a chuckle came out of him. "*You* know.

"Anyway, I can't seem to settle anywhere. I was in England, and after—I went to France, and then Canada. Found a couple of—demons—in Vancouver, managed to deal with them, decided I'd see what else I would find. I'm trying to recover some of the books and artifacts, too, that we had—that we lost. Rebuild, if you will. That's what brought me here, looking up some of the local dealers. Stanhope up in Vancouver put me on to Tobey Cawber, said he might have a couple of the things I'm looking for. Thought I might go to New Orleans next."

"What *are* you looking for?" Angel asked, as Fred said at the same time, "Tobey Cawber? He's no longer with us."

O'Flaherty chose to answer Fred first, as a gentleman might. "Died? It must have been very recent. I'm sorry to hear it. What happened?"

What he meant, of course, was, *What killed him?*

"We're not entirely certain he's dead," Wesley said. "He's gone, that's all. Been missing for several weeks. Stanhope might not have realized it when you last spoke to him." Wesley had helped himself to a cup of coffee. As if he belonged there with the rest of them, Angel thought. Hoped.

"Disappeared?" O'Flaherty said with one eyebrow arched high.

"That's right," Angel confirmed. He was listening to the steady pulses of the humans in the room, the slightly fast beat of Gunn's heart that said he was still in some pain, though he'd never admit it; the solid regular rhythm of Wes's, Cordy's, Fred's—and the little quiver in their visitor's. Maybe it was fear.

"I'm very sorry to hear that," O'Flaherty repeated, with quiet emphasis.

"A wasted trip, then?" Wesley said. He was leaning now against the counter, observing, the coffee cup set aside.

O'Flaherty shrugged. "I hope not. Perhaps I'll look around a bit." He hesitated. "Although I understand that's what—Angel Investigations—does. I don't mean to step on any toes."

"I think we can manage to coordinate our activities," Wesley said dryly.

Angel smiled. "More coffee?"

"Thanks, I'd like that."

Or maybe he's lying about something. I wonder what. The man was definitely concealing something, in any case.

That didn't have to be bad, necessarily. But it might be.

"If you've taken after your father's interests," Wes continued—and Angel noted with interest the jolt in O'Flaherty's heartbeat—"perhaps you'd like to see the small library we've put together here. Nothing like what he had put together back home, of course."

"Your father?" Fred inquired.

"My father was the librarian for the Council," O'Flaherty said, accepting the refilled cup. His tone was almost dismissive.

"Gabriel O'Flaherty was one of the most brilliant researchers and teachers the Watchers Council ever had," Wes amplified. "It was a tragic loss, and I should have offered my condolences sooner, old man."

"Thank you," the other man said softly. There was a small silence, and he put the coffee down untasted, the china clicking sharply against the polished wood of the table. "I'd like very much to see what you have, if you don't mind."

"Of course." Wes and O'Flaherty stood, and Wesley led the visitor to the back room, leaving the rest of Angel Investigations looking at one another with speculation writ large on their faces.

"Well, that was interesting." Typically, Cordelia was the first to break the silence. "I wonder what he's *really* here for?"

"Well, he sure wasn't planning on meeting you," Gunn said, watching Angel.

"No," Angel agreed. "Whatever it is, I don't think it has anything to do with me. Which is kind of refreshing, you know?"

"Then why did he look up Wesley? They weren't friends before, that was pretty obvious."

Gunn grinned. "Yeah, our man Wes punked him out pretty good, didn't he?"

"Maybe," Fred mused, "he was just looking for somebody familiar, even if he didn't exactly like him. It sounds like he lost everybody. Even his father. If you lose enough, even the people you really don't like start to look like good memories after a while."

She was thinking about the years she had spent in Pylea, Angel realized.

Maybe it was true. Maybe Adrian O'Flaherty was just looking for one of the few familiar faces left from the world he'd grown up in.

But he was holding something back, too, and that bothered the vampire. It might not have anything to do with *him*, but he didn't want it to have anything to do with Wesley, either, and that was going to be a little more difficult.

He strolled behind the counter and found something to busy his hands, and listened, shamelessly eavesdropping as a vampire could. When he happened to look up, he saw Cordy, Fred, and Gunn watching him, knowing exactly what he was doing. He shrugged a little. He wasn't above using the strength that being a vampire gave him; he wasn't going to waste the other gifts, either.

"Amazing," O'Flaherty was saying. Pages ruffled; cloth whispered as one man or the other pivoted. A soft slap as a book was closed. Leather sighed as one volume was replaced on a shelf, another withdrawn for examination. "I don't think I've ever seen a copy of this outside of Father's private library."

Was that an accusation?

No. Honest envy.

"It's Angel's," Wesley admitted. "Not mine. He actually got it from Cawber, I believe."

Light footsteps crossing the room. "Are all these Angelus—Angel's, then?"

"Not all. Some of them are mine. Some belong to Fred. She's beginning to pick up on research." Wood creaked. Wes was sitting in the old chair at the end of the desk, then, watching as the other man examined the shelves. Made sense. That's where Angel would have positioned himself, too, so he could see exactly which books got attention and which ones were skipped over as not worth a look.

O'Flaherty's voice dropped, as if that would have made the slightest difference. "It must be a trifle unsettling. Being a Watcher. Working with—"

Angel could visualize the jerk of the head toward the door. He continued listening, patiently. What a Watcher thought didn't bother him.

The pause before Wesley answered did bother him a bit.

"I have worked with Angel for some years," Wesley said at last. "I think we know what to expect from each other. We know what each of us is capable of by now."

Including, Angel realized with a wry smile, supernatural hearing. Wesley knew perfectly well he was standing out here and listening to every word of the conversation.

Across the room, Gunn stirred, wondering, then settled back. The phone rang, and Cordy went off to answer it.

"And I haven't been a Watcher for several years either," Wesley continued. He didn't add, *There are no more Watchers,* but he might as well have.

O'Flaherty didn't respond, at least not in any

way that made any noise, for some moments. Then he said, "Have you heard from anyone else?"

A tiny sound that was probably a shrug. "Giles, occasionally. If you mean anyone with an official Council connection, no. You *did* still have a connection, didn't you? Other than your father?"

"One's father on the Council doesn't guarantee a connection, does it?" Another answer that didn't answer, a reference to shared history.

Quiet laughter, not entirely a happy sound. Sound of paper shoved to one side. He was probably sitting on the edge of the desk now. Fred and Gunn were getting a little tired of staring at Angel, and had gone back to finishing up food, finding other things to occupy themselves until they could discover the details.

Angel continued to listen; a vampire was a predator, and predators were patient.

"Yes, well, sometimes they wondered about that, I'm sure," O'Flaherty went on. "I was still a member, yes. Sheer luck I wasn't—"

An abrupt silence, easily interpreted as Englishmen demonstrating the art of the stiff upper lip.

"Well, you're here now," Wesley said, offering an abrupt change of subject. "And as I recall, you were always rather good at chemistry. I actually came over here today to help make up a new supply of d'nuluath ointment for the group—care to pitch in? I could use an extra pair of hands."

"The group." Angel could easily imagine their visitor shaking his head over that. "I know you said this Angel Investigations looks into supernatural questions, but really, Pryce—a demon? A vampire—*that* vampire? Good lord, man."

"Can you think of a better qualified team?" Wesley asked dryly. "At any rate, we manage."

And he hasn't even mentioned Connor, Angel thought, and was momentarily grateful that his son had chosen to do some exploring up the coast for a few days. Some complications were just too complicated to get into. The Watchers would never have believed that a vampire could have a son— that two vampires, the notorious Darla and Angelus, could have a *human* son. Even if Angelus, the demon, was firmly under the control of Angel, the vampire with a soul, it would still be flatly dismissed as impossible.

"Something funny?" Gunn asked, his voice pitched very low. He had left his chair and come over to the counter to stand beside Angel. His merely human senses didn't allow him to hear what was going on, however, and the frustration steamed out of him.

Angel smiled. "I was just thinking what Wes's Watchers Council would have made of Connor."

"They're not his Council," Gunn pointed out. The Council had booted him out in disgrace for failing to control Faith when that Slayer had gone rogue, and there was still some bitterness left. Then, almost as an afterthought, he added, "I guess they're not anybody's anymore. But you're right. From what English has said, adaptability isn't—wasn't—one of their strong points."

Angel nodded and went back to listening.

Wesley had said, "*We* manage." That part was good, really good. He'd like to think that he'd apologized to Wesley for the rage, for the misunderstanding, for the months of cold silence between them. He'd like to think that the books were closed on all the issues between them; that, just as Wes had told O'Flaherty, they knew each other. But that knife cut both ways, and Angel still felt guilty about it. He wondered if there could ever again be total, unquestioning trust on either side. Wesley would always be the man who had stolen Angel's son. Angel would always be the—man—who had tried to strangle Wes as he lay helpless in his hospital bed.

But he had to hope. His whole existence, after all, was based on hoping that doing the right thing would eventually make a difference.

And things *were* better than they had been. *Much* better.

"So do you want to help?" Wes was asking his visitor. "Shouldn't take more than a few hours."

O'Flaherty took the olive branch gratefully. "Certainly. Glad to help out, brush up on some of the old—"

Cordelia screamed.

Angel spun around to see Cordelia collapsing, Lorne moving across the room in a futile attempt to get to her, and was at her side before she could hit the ground.

"Kids—no—" She screamed again and convulsed, and by that time both Wesley and O'Flaherty were out of the office and O'Flaherty was reaching for a cell phone.

"No, don't," Fred was telling him. "No ambulance."

"But she's having seizures," he said, obviously confused.

"It's all right," Lorne told him. "She'll be okay. Cordy, honey, what did you see?"

By that time Cordelia was sagging in Angel's arms, breathing hard. "The kids again. They're in some place with trees, a park. Horses—" Her eyes widened. "I know where it was! I auditioned for a commercial there! It's the horse place at Griffin Park. Angel, it's out in the open." She swallowed hard. "There's a thing with way too many teeth, and those kids—"

"Perhaps we'll do the ointment later this afternoon," Wesley said. He looked over at Gunn, who was gamely swaying to his feet. "Don't be an utter fool, Charles. Angel, if it's in the open, you can't risk it. Cordelia, are you up to it? Fred? O'Flaherty, let's go."

"Keep in touch," Angel growled. Wes was being brisk and efficient again.

"Yes," he responded, and they were out the door.

They had made it all the way down to the Buena Vista exit before O'Flaherty got it about Cordelia and the visions. They were inside the park and cruising by the time he understood that this was pretty much the kind of thing they did most of the time, except that it more often happened at night, and they had the additional advantage of a vampire on their side.

Unfortunately, this was a fairly typical late-summer California day: warm, sunny, and guaranteed to give even a vampire with the best of intentions a terminal sunburn. So they were on their own, split into pairs: Fred and O'Flaherty walking the barns and shed rows, and Wesley and Cordelia scanning the arenas and fields, trying to spot something that looked like the area that she'd seen in her vision and be discreet about the various hardware they were lugging about.

Meanwhile, back at the Hyperion Hotel, both Angel and Gunn were cursing the respective disabilities that prevented them from participating in the chase.

Cursing, however, wasn't going to kill any demons, at least not this kind of cursing. Gunn quickly gave it up in disgust.

"You really think these kids are a serious problem?" he asked Angel, trying to distract the vampire from his frustrated pacing back and forth across the lobby. "I mean, they're just kids, right?"

Angel stopped and let go a long sigh with breath he didn't have—a sign of exasperation, nothing else. "I'm not thinking of the *kids* as a problem, exactly. I don't want them to get killed. I don't want them to *become* a problem—hell, everybody was a kid once. I just want to get out there—I want to be in it, not back here. Drives me crazy."

Gunn chuckled, shifted his arm, winced. "Know what you mean." He shook his head. "Still, this is the second time Cordy's got a vision about them. Powers must be worried."

"Maybe they just get into trouble a *lot*. The first time, we got there before most of those kids got into the building. Maybe they didn't get the message that they're dealing with something bigger than they are."

"Or maybe they got the message and they like the idea," Gunn said glumly.

"That's what I'm afraid of too." Angel went back to pacing.

CHAPTER SIX

Sunlight. Blue skies. Young women and horses.

Fred Burkle thought they were all out of their minds.

She'd read *The Black Stallion* and *Misty of Chincoteague* and *National Velvet* when she was a kid, trying to figure out what it was about horses that got all the other girls her age to go crazy. She'd even dutifully gone on pony rides. Still, she didn't get it. While other little girls begged for a horse of their very own, a pony for Christmas, Fred knew that *Equus caballus* was a big, smelly animal with big teeth and big feet. If you gave it an apple, it would probably take your hand with it, and it was scared of its own shadow. When it panicked, a thousand pounds of witless terror would either step on you or knock you over while it tried to get away from a paper bag blowing in the wind. And there were far more efficient ways of consuming fuel to move from place to place, and the mess—well, okay, it was more biodegradable, but that was the only plus she could think of.

So she let the stranger walk closer to the stalls and glance inside, and avoided the heads stuck over the doors.

"Cordy said she saw trees," she said at last. "We should probably go look over there." She pointed to a grassy, shaded area beyond the stables. Some of the round fenced-in sections had horses, but most were empty.

"I suppose the paddocks are more likely."

Fred shot the Englishman a suspicious look, but if he was laughing at her, he didn't show it. She breathed a sigh of relief to get away from the stalls, with their piles of crap and puddles, and nearly walked into a brown horse. Its rider looked down at her as if she were some kind of idiot. Well, *she* wasn't sitting on something that would probably buck her off at any opportunity! O'Flaherty caught her by the arm and pulled her out of the way.

There were quite a few people out there—more than she'd expected. Somebody was chasing a horse in a circle over there—the only thing keeping the animal from running away was the rope on its face. She couldn't see why it didn't just drag the woman. There were two or three other riders, and at least four people just standing around talking, one of them showing the others some kind of leather strap thing. They all seemed deeply impressed.

"I hope Cordy and Wes are having better luck than we are," she said. "How are we supposed to locate a demon in all this?"

"You're right," he said. "It wouldn't be happening here. Pryce would know that too." Traffic had separated their little convoy, and O'Flaherty and Fred had arrived to find Wes's car already in the lot.

O'Flaherty paused and thought for a moment, then approached one of the riders, looking up and smiling. It was a charming smile, Fred thought. She wouldn't trust it for a moment. "Excuse me."

The rider probably had had her brains scrambled from falling off too many times. Even though she was wearing a helmet, she was smiling back at the guy. "Yes?"

Fred hung back at a safe distance, watching; the horse was actually rather pretty, almost pure white, with really big brown eyes, and not nearly as huge as some of them—but still, it was a horse. Not to be trusted.

"I was wondering—I'd heard that one of the jump fields, or something, was closed today, and I couldn't remember which one it was. I'm afraid I'm a bit confused. Can you help me?"

He was really pouring on the accent, too, Fred thought. It was much more pronounced than it had been earlier, back at the hotel.

The rider shrugged. "Sorry, don't do jumping. I'm strictly dressage. Jessie might know." She turned around in the saddle and yelled, "Yo, Jess! Something closed today?"

Fred took another step back, sure that the white horse would shriek and start a rodeo as a result of the sudden noise. But no. The animal just stood there, and there was O'Flaherty, gently stroking its neck and making admiring comments. The horse was apparently just as susceptible to charm as its rider was. It lowered its head and sighed deeply, obviously in love.

Jessie was riding the towering brown horse she'd nearly walked into. How she'd missed it, Fred could not imagine. She yelled back something incomprehensible, which apparently O'Flaherty understood, and after a minute or two he nodded, thanked them both, and set off in a direction quite opposite to the one in which they'd been pointing in a leisurely stroll.

"Where are we going?" she asked. "I thought they said the one that was closed was back that way."

"We go in the direction they expect us to," he said as they swung around the back of a barn, followed by an infectious grin. "*Now* we go in the direction we want to." They doubled back, picking up the pace.

Halfway there, Fred began to see far more trees and far fewer people.

Three quarters of the way, she spotted Cordelia's favorite scarf, a bright splotch of red and gold silk against the green grass.

And just past a final row of trees, the search was over.

Ahead, a cornered and terrified horse was rearing its front legs and kicking savagely against a blur of red-orange creatures that clung to its haunches. A bunch of high school kids were scrambling away from their broken summoning circle. Cordelia was beating off one of the things that crouched in front of her. And finally, Wes was trying to stay out of the maddened horse's way while pulling two demons off a teenager who'd fallen.

The little red-orange demons were all teeth, short fur, and a dozen legs with sharp hooklike claws. Fred didn't want to look at the torn bodies of those less lucky. Terrified screaming filled the air.

Fred took a firm grip on her wakizashi and ran into battle.

O'Flaherty yelled to Wes and started swinging a sword he'd produced from somewhere—no one had seen him take it out of the arms cabinet, but its source certainly wasn't as important as how well he used it, which was very well indeed. Wes stepped away from the kids and let his former colleague whack at the demons while he started casting a spell to close the dimensional vortex. The little demons would try to stare at you with hot red eyes, freeze you with a look, and if one of them could get its teeth into you, a bunch of them would swarm you; the trick was to get them while they were trying to nail you with that look, or hit them in midair, because if they got their teeth in you, well, by the looks of the bodies, you got covered in molten fur. She hoped the kids got away. She was too busy to look and see.

A hole shimmered in the side of the adjacent earth bank, gray and foggy, and Fred risked a look in between an executed one-two piranha demon's slice 'n' hack. The hole stretched wider, and it billowed, bulged. More little demons scampered out, and she and Cordy and O'Flaherty chopped and smashed at them as fast as they could. The horse had stopped screaming; she didn't dare look back in that direction. The more horrific sounds of tearing flesh and chewing were coming from that direction now. It was better to focus on Wes, who was steadily chanting, in Old Sumerian or Urdu. She hoped his buddy was keeping the demons off him long enough to let him finish the spell.

And quickly.

Fred looked up to see six hooked, shiny silver claws, each as long as the average scythe, slice through the portal's mist and curve around the edge of the hole, flexing as if to get a better grip on reality. Her reality. She took the hilt of her short

ANGEL

sword in both hands, lifted it high overhead, and
brought it down on the claws as hard as she could.

The tempered steel fell into seven neat slices
that would have made Martha Stewart proud.

Fred looked down at the stub that remained in
her hands, at the claws flexing less than two feet
from her nose, squeaked, and fell backward.

Something grabbed her shoulders and dragged,
and she screamed and twisted, only to hear Cordy
hiss in her ear, "I already have a headache you
would not be*lieve*. I don't need you squalling in my
ear. Get up already. I only do ten-foot hauls."

Fred started to turn to respond, had just rested
the palms of her hands behind her on the slippery
grass and bent her knees to shove herself back to
her feet, when something landed on her chest and
knocked her back down again. She found herself
staring down a purple-black gullet ringed with
rows and rows of teeth that widened in eagerness
as the furry orange piranha reared back on her
chest to get a really good bite out of her face.

And then *something* snarled, and she could have
sworn she heard the furry piranha give a startled
yip as it was scooped up and off of her, its claws
ripping her best blouse to shreds in the process—a
fair exchange, considering—and the little monster
went flying right through the misty circle that
marked the dimensional opening . . . where of
course it hit whatever was trying to come through

from the other side, and bounced right back out again. But it apparently had the brains to know when it was outclassed, because it spun around and scrambled back. If it had had a tail it would have been tucked between its multiple legs.

Fred was back on her feet by this time and searching for something else she could use as a weapon. Meanwhile her rescuer, heavily swathed in a long coat, wide-brimmed hat, gloves, boots, and some kind of weird veil that protected the back of his neck, was tromping all over the grass and picking up swarming reddies and giving them the heave-ho.

Fred knew only one person who had to cover himself up completely to go out in the midday sun. The boss was here.

Every once in a while the little red demons would squirm around and try to bite him. And he'd snarl, and sometimes he'd just—

Rip them in half. And then go find more to maim and destroy.

Fred swallowed hard and stepped back against a tree to protect her back, picked up a handy branch, and kept out of the way. Cordy, she noticed, had decided to do much the same thing. O'Flaherty was still sweeping a circle around Wes with that long flamberge blade, handling it with amazing dexterity. Wes was still reciting, ignoring the carnage around him, focusing on the pulsing vortex and the claws, which were now matched by a second set on the other side of the circle.

And a third set on the top. This was really *not* good, Fred thought. The claws were pushing the portal's walls out, while Wes's counterspelling was pushing them in, trying to close the vortex. Meanwhile, the rest of the little red-orange demons were either working their way through—literally—the various scattered bodies, or were circling the survivors, looking for a chance to pick them off. The kids who had started this mess were either dead or gone by this time, most likely. So, no survivors there.

Well, she thought giddily, you couldn't technically call Angel a "survivor." But he was definitely a combatant. He and O'Flaherty were the only combatants left, in fact, and O'Flaherty was just about to fall on his sword in sheer exhaustion. One of the little demons sprang at his back; he spun to chop at it, and only a supernatural quickness kept Angel from losing his head. For an instant, the vampire held the former Watcher's wrist in a bone-cracking grasp, the wavy blade dull with gore over their heads, and then he stepped back just in time to snatch yet another little monster out of the air and toss it away.

Wes kept chanting. His voice was getting raw. Fred thought she could see a snout—at least she hoped it was a snout, and not eyes—on the other side of the mist, coming closer.

There were fewer of the little demons now, and

they were focusing on Wes, as if they intuitively knew that he was the one they needed to distract. Every once in a while a new one would sneak out of the mist and make a dive for him, too, dodging around Angel and O'Flaherty. They were quicker, less stupid about it, harder to catch. At one point, three of them had whipped around Angel, when Cordy, who was against a tree to Fred's right, yelled, "Wes! Behind you!"

O'Flaherty jerked around to see two piranhas poised to jump Wes from behind. Wes didn't stop, but he stuttered. While O'Flaherty lunged for the demons, he knocked Wes sprawling, and sent the grimoire he was using fluttering across the gory swamp that used to be a lawn. The vortex ripped.

Something very large started through, roaring.

Angel roared back.

The little demons were all tiny claws and big mouths. This thing had very big claws and a very, very big mouth. It took up the entire diameter of the vortex, and struggled to pop itself through, mostly because its mouth was open and its teeth were bared.

Wesley, sprawled on his belly, paged frantically to find his place in the vortex-closing spell.

Angel looked around to find something appropriate to fill an open mouth, picked up the remains of a thirteen-hundred-pound heavy hunter, and all but rammed it down the demon's throat—saddle, bridle, stirrups, and all. Wes dug into his pocket for a container of something and tossed it overhand like a grenade into the mist of the vortex as he finished the final sentences of the spell; and the interdimensional vortex snapped decisively shut. The little demons who had survived so far ran for the trees, for the other jumps, for anything they could hide behind. Riding in the horse park was going to be more of an adventure than usual for a while.

From the shelter of a ditch bank, fifty yards away— as far as he'd been able to get before prying loose a baby monster chewing on his leg and bashing it with a piece of the jump—Emilio lay watching, mouth agape, as the guy in the hat and coat picked up the dead horse like it was *nothing* and heaved it at the demon in the vortex. The guy must be as strong as Superman! And then the other guy, who had been doing the chanting, casting the spell from the book, threw something he couldn't see at the thing, and the circular hole into somewhere else was gone. Just like that.

Emilio licked his lips. Now *that* was power.

He didn't know if the rest of the books he'd taken from Cawber's would let him do anything like that, but he wanted to try.

And *then* let his dad, or Mrs. Grey, or the jocks at school try to bust his chops. He'd show *them*. He'd show all of them.

It was too bad about Victers, though. She'd believed in him before anybody else had, and she'd been pretty. Before she got eaten.

An hour and a half later, they were back at the Hyperion Hotel, binding their various wounds. It had taken a while to try to identify the victims, and Angel wanted to find as many of the little red guys as possible before they left.

They'd finally convinced him that defeating Big Mama was a win, and he should take it as such. Now they were sharing war stories.

"*Salt?*" Cordy stared at Wesley. "You had to throw *salt* at it?"

Wes arched an eyebrow at her. "I believe that's what I said. Sea salt, to be exact."

"Well, if that was all it took, why were you taking all that time with the spell?" she demanded. "Did you see what those little monsters were doing? I ruined a Dolce and Gabbana dress out there!"

Cordy opened her mouth to say something else, but suddenly thought better of it when she took notice of the expression on Wes's face.

"The spell was required to enchant the salt," O'Flaherty said softly. "That particular spell is notoriously difficult under the best of conditions." He paused. "Actually, there are no 'best' conditions. The ritual has to be performed in the presence of the demon to be exorcised. The timing required generally means you're dead before you can finish it." He passed a mortar full of dried sage leaves and Toshet demon hairs over to Wes, along with a marble pestle, and dribbled olive oil onto a polished metal plate. Gunn watched, fascinated, as he picked up a chef's knife and began chopping celery. That was an awfully big knife for celery, he thought. And it was just amazing how close magickal herbology looked like a luncheon salad. He wondered if the size of the knife had some mystical significance, or if it was just easier to chop vegetables with than a paring knife.

Wes nodded at Angel as he ground the dried ingredients. "If you hadn't thrown that horse at it, we'd all have been finished."

Angel shrugged. "Aren't we all just brimming with the team spirit? Still doesn't tell us who the kids were, where they got such powerful spells, and *why*."

"Couldn't they just be kids?" Fred asked. "Really dumb kids. Trying to be big shots, I mean?"

"Well, if they were, they succeeded pretty darned well," Cordy pointed out. "I could sure believe it. I mean, when we got there, they looked pretty wanna-be. I don't think the oldest one was more than sixteen or so. But those spells were pretty mature. They got their hands on some heavy-duty stuff."

"And they couldn't handle it," Wes pointed out. "They could open the vortex, summon the demon, but they couldn't control it. They obviously didn't have any training. And now they're all dead."

"Do you know that for sure?" O'Flaherty asked, passing minced celery over to him. "Some could have gotten away, you know. Or perhaps not all of the young people involved were present today."

"That's true," Fred agreed. "We don't know if we're finished with this or not. All we know is that the ones who were there when Wes was done are dead."

"Which brings me back to the Gilman collection," Angel said. "That's the centerpiece of the auction, but as I said, there are a lot of other stores that decided to put some of their rarer pieces in. It's attracting collectors from all over the world. If some of these kids escaped today, and they somehow have a line on rare books and spells, maybe—"

"Do you really expect teenagers to show up to bid?" Wesley asked, pausing for a moment as he powdered the herbs. "At Melchior's, the biggest auctioneers of the occult in the Western Hemisphere?"

"And would they still want to play with magick, after today?" Gunn asked.

"Power is addictive," O'Flaherty said quietly, leaning on the hilt of the big knife as it rested point down on the counter. "Almost as addictive as knowledge . . . which one could argue is a form of power." Wesley passed him more stalks of celery, and he went back to work.

"I don't know *what* I expect," Angel admitted. "But we need to know who's at this thing. They're having it in daylight and in the open to keep most of the demonic elements out, but we all know that's not really going to help. They'll have agents. But if you can go see who's bidding on what, and make the connections, maybe we can figure out ahead of time where trouble's going to show up."

"Boy, wouldn't *that* be a switch," Cordelia said dryly.

"You know what I mean. I've got the invitation; you might as well make use of it. I certainly can't go." Angel wouldn't be able to get away with the all-enveloping coat and hat and gloves in front of the security at an auction like this one.

"And maybe if somebody buys some major mojo and takes it *out* of our territory, that wouldn't be bad to know either," Gunn observed. He was still watching the knife chopping the celery into pieces so small as to be almost mush, now. "What makes this goop purple?"

Wes smiled grimly. "You don't really want to know that." He reached under the counter for measuring spoons, and a set of clay jars whose contents he sniffed; nodded approvingly; and began mixing the dry ingredients into a bowl.

"So I expect you're planning on going to this auction," Angel asked O'Flaherty, who had added a set of red twigs into the oily celery-mush.

O'Flaherty smiled. "I wouldn't miss it for the world," he said, stirring the mixture. "I told Wesley last night, that was one reason I came down here. He may not have mentioned it, but my father was the librarian for the Watchers Council. I was brought up among books. There's a special attraction to them."

"Oh, yes!" Fred glowed in response. "I know what you mean. I can just get *lost* in a good book. I can get so absorbed in reading that time flies by. Have you ever looked at the number of pages left to read and wished there could be more because a book was just so *interesting*? Or stay up all night reading and not even know it until the sun came up? Or—"

She realized suddenly that they were all staring at her. Babbling again. She blushed and shut up.

Wes was smiling, that private look in his eyes that made her feel off-guard, and Gunn was looking at her as if she were a little bit alien, but somebody he still wanted, and that made her feel awkward, too, and she hated feeling awkward.

"I do know what you mean," O'Flaherty said. "My father was like that. We used to say you could set a bomb off and he'd never—" His lips tightened, and he focused on the work in front of him, his hands quick and efficient as he mixed ingredients.

"I'm sorry for your loss," Angel said quietly.

"Thank you," O'Flaherty muttered, and suddenly he blinked in shock and looked up at Angel, laying the mortar aside. "I'm sorry, this is just very strange."

The two of them looked at each other for a long moment, vampire and Watcher, trying to adjust to a world in which nothing was in its proper place, where every expected behavior was cancelled and replaced by a new set of common courtesies.

Who are you really? they asked each other. *What do you really want?*

And what is it going to cost me to find out?

"So what is this 'Egan estate'?" O'Flaherty asked the next day as he slipped on a pair of sunglasses and draped an elbow out the passenger window of Wes's car. They'd decided to go to the auction together, and Wesley had picked O'Flaherty up at the hotel immediately after lunch. It had given O'Flaherty the whole morning to do some more research on his own little project, which was fine with him. The possibilities were narrowing down nicely.

He watched the passing scenery, uncertain tourists consulting maps, and natives in sunglasses with tiny, useless lenses, jogging with casual efficiency to the private rhythms of earphones. They were driving through an expensive commercial district in Beverly Hills, filled with stores and tourist traps, everything from upscale clothing and jewelry to furniture and housewares, dance studios and restaurants, stores selling tea and tofu, crystals and diamonds. Palm trees lined the streets, their leaves striping the blue air. The sun was hot through a haze of smoke and pollution, the air acrid from engine exhaust and the smell of late-summer fires that swept the hills and ate into the dry paradise that was Los Angeles. "Who was Egan? Sorcerer? Vampire? Millionaire dilettante?"

"I'm not certain, but I believe he was a wealthy eccentric with odd research interests. The fact that they're having the auction there, however, may not be related to those interests."

"I don't believe in coincidences. Do you?"

Wes didn't bother to answer.

They left the shopping district behind as Wes sent the car up a winding, narrow road into the hills, past driveways with heavy gates, and stone walls. Once or twice Wes had to swerve sharply to avoid a vehicle coming from the other direction. O'Flaherty turned in his seat to stare out the back window. "Bugger me, was that a *Lancia*?"

"Probably. We'll be lucky if we're not Humvee'd off this road." He made a sharp turn onto an even smaller lane. Oleander branches scraped both sides of the car. "We'll be lucky if we're not *skateboarded* off *this* road."

"I thought you'd been here before."

"I don't move in these circles. I know about

some of the places in this auction, but I've never been up here before."

"How do you know the way, then?"

"Angel briefed me this morning. His directions were very explicit."

"He's been here, then?"

"One assumes so." Another abrupt turn. Two hundred yards down an overgrown gravel driveway, the shadowy overhanging trees abruptly disappeared, and they were pulling into an open driveway with an elaborate wrought-iron gate, twelve feet high, set in stone columns with crouching griffins leering down at them.

"Lovely," O'Flaherty said. "Now what?"

Behind them, a Jaguar XE pulled out of the shadows and idled behind them.

A voice from one of the griffins said, "Identity?"

"Wyndam-Pryce, Auction Esoterica."

"Pass."

The gates opened silently, and they drove through. O'Flaherty turned to watch, and reported, "They closed behind us. Apparently everyone has to be admitted individually. I wonder what happens if one doesn't have the password?"

Wesley laughed. "Considering the contents of this auction?"

They continued up a paved driveway toward a house—no, a fortress—that could have been transplanted from the Tuscan hills. A red tile roof topped whitewashed walls. A large open area in front of the majestic building was nearly filled with automobiles of all descriptions. They could see several dozen people clustered on a balcony that stretched the entire length of the house.

"What do you suppose we'll find?" asked O'Flaherty.

"Other than what was in the catalog? I have no idea," Wesley said uneasily. "That's what we're here to find out."

He parked the car and they got out and started toward the front door, dodging the Jaguar that was cruising up and down the rows of vehicles looking for a space.

"I thought I had allowed plenty of time to look things over before the auction begins. It doesn't start for another four hours. Look around. We barely got here in time."

The only thing that could be said about most of the attendees, Wes thought, was that at least they were human. Although he'd met some demons he liked better than the humans gathered in the gardens of the Egan mansion. There were perhaps fifty people, total, milling around the pool and the refreshments tables.

He and O'Flaherty had passed through at least two different scrying portals, and he was sure there were more he *hadn't* spotted. Evidently the Melchior's auction house was serious about catering strictly to the human trade.

"Who are the earnest young things in business suits?" O'Flaherty inquired, jutting his chin at the objects of his inquiry over a rather decent light gin. Wes considered it to be too early for the hard stuff; he was sticking to orange juice for the moment. He suspected the lavish refreshments set out by the free-form garden pool were designed to loosen wallets, and his was rather thin at the moment.

"Wolfram and Hart associates, I suspect. They have quite a library. Probably looking for something in particular to add to their collection."

O'Flaherty nodded, but Wes noticed that his eyes continued to watch the Wolfram & Hart representatives.

"Over by the bougainvillea are a pair from Whitwaterstrand's. Occult art house. The lady in white is a private collector. We exorcised a few Nimmi imps who had infested a vase she purchased last month. There are half a dozen buyers for the more select stores up and down the coast, and as many more for the . . . less select."

"And those over there?"

Standing under a mimosa were two men dressed in long, sacklike brown robes, with knotted white ropes pinching the robes to their bellies and hanging nearly to the ground. As they turned away from O'Flaherty and Wesley, the sun gleamed off the bald spots shaved into the crowns of their heads.

"They look rather like Franciscan monks, don't they? I've no idea who they are. From out of town, I'd guess."

"Well. I'll look around, shall I?"

Wesley stood back and watched as O'Flaherty moved out and around the pool, smiling at and skimming through the various groups of people. He was good at the light socializing, the quick introductions. He didn't know what O'Flaherty thought he was accomplishing, though. Making contacts?

Meanwhile, Wesley was supposed to be looking for teenage wanna-be wizards, and he hadn't spotted anyone under twenty-five at best; in fact, he and O'Flaherty were probably the youngest people present. He kept out of the ebb and flow but moved around enough to be a little less obvious about his survey.

He had been standing under the orange trees, shading his eyes from the light reflecting off the water, for nearly half an hour when the chief auctioneer's assistant came out on the deck above the garden. Melchior's might cater to the human trade, but the auction house itself was staffed entirely with demons. The assistant was nearly translucent in the sunlight, and didn't need an amplifier when it spoke: "Ladies and gentlemen, may I have your attention, please."

The murmuring around the pool stopped as everyone turned to listen.

"We have quite a number of items for your consideration today. Some of them are job lots that we have collected for your inspection in the next garden. Others are rather more exclusive and have been described in our catalog, which was transmitted to you electronically a month ago.

"We will begin the auction of the job lots in two and a half hours. The catalog auction is expected to begin at seven o'clock precisely. You are welcome to handle the objects in the job lots, but we caution you not to inadvertently move an item from one box into another. They are magickally attached to their particular boxes, and I'm afraid that rather embarrassing alarms will be set off. If you win one of the lots, please remind me to disengage the box before you leave the premises— I'm afraid the consequences will be rather distressing otherwise."

A ripple of uncomfortable laughter crossed the garden.

"Because of the large number of objects offered today, we will be conducting our sale in series: Those of you who are particularly interested in books will find them offered last. We will begin with some particularly interesting magickal objects with considerable historical interest—"

"And absolutely no occult potential," O'Flaherty commented sarcastically beside Wesley, sotto voce. It was obvious from the expressions on the faces of the others in the crowd that he was not the only one to think so.

"We will continue with several potions and individual spells. Melchior's makes no warranty, of course, as to the efficacy of any items on offer."

"Naturally not," grumbled O'Flaherty.

Wesley gave him an irritated look. He was more interested in what the glassine demon had to say than he was in O'Flaherty's cynical commentary. What had the man come for, if he thought so little of the items on offer at the auction?

"We will then take a break for refreshments, and continue with several objects of power that have been described in detail in our catalog, and finally the rare and precious grimoires that Melchior's is known for. These *objets de puissance mystical* and *livres occultes* may be viewed at your leisure until the auction begins, at which time you will be requested, of course, to take your seats.

"We will conclude with the auction of the job lots.

"You are now welcome to enter the second garden. Please leave your food and drinks here. You will be issued your bidding numbers as you enter the garden." The assistant raised one translucent hand and gestured elegantly to a rose arbor that arched over one corner gate. As he did so, the gate swung ajar.

Wesley Wyndam-Pryce had been a compulsive reader since he was a small child, though his subjects of choice were probably not to be found in the checkout lines of most local grocery stores. Still, when one is drawn irresistibly to books, bookstores, book sales, *rare book auctions*—like any addict, one inevitably finds something to feed, however temporarily, the need.

The rose arbor led to a short flight of steps into the "second garden" of the Egan estate—an open lawn surrounded by more roses, a riot of reds and pinks and gold. Set in front of the rosebushes, a series of long tables covered with functional green baize displayed the items on offer. In the center of the circle of tables, rows of chairs faced the auctioneer's podium, currently empty, and a smaller table beside it.

Nearest the entrance steps were the mentioned job lot items—cardboard boxes, some of them in tatters, showing considerable history as shipping material, or starting their careers in a grocery store warehouse. These were open for inspection. In front of each box was a number identifying its lot. The boxes contained a jumble of hardbound and paperback books, odd bits of crystal, amulets, empty vials missing their stoppers—junk, clearly, in the eyes of the auctioneers and of the discerning buyers who swept past them without a second sneering glance.

Each table closer to the podium held more individual items; the guards, all Tekhash demons, Wesley noted, were focused on the last two on either side. Presumably those held treasures someone might find it worthwhile to risk a curse or two to steal. No one in his right mind, or even considerably out of it, would consider challenging a Tekhash; instead of arms, they had a set of four muscular tentacles writhing from each shoulder, and each one held a weapon. Their eight eyes, diamond-clear and flat, circled their skulls. Their "legs" were also tentacles that dug into the ground and anchored them when they didn't want to move, and propelled them across almost any terrain faster than a cheetah when they did. Under most conditions Tekhash demons were mild-mannered, as demons went, and not inclined to be aggressive, but that was because they could afford to be.

He noted that O'Flaherty joined most of the rest of the buyers, heading immediately to the mid-range tables and working his way slowly toward the podium. Wes hung back, keeping in mind that he was supposed to be looking for things out of place, or for someone who might buy something for a teenager. What that might look like, he had no idea; it wasn't as if the kids were talking someone into buying them an illegal beer, or cigarettes, after all.

The Wolfram & Hart associates were concentrating on various arcana, one of them pointing out to another an item that was, according to the catalog, "A nearly complete example of Sumerian death magick amulets." The catalog went on to list the amulets included; what it failed to mention was that the ones that were missing were the keys required to make the rest functional. Those, it turned out, were offered separately, at a table higher up in the circle.

"Probably a good idea," O'Flaherty said, returning to Wesley's side. "One wouldn't want the whole package in one place, now would one? Too tempting to try out the merchandise."

Wesley glanced over at the smaller man. "They're still missing the Baal's Eye. Without that, most of the more interesting conjurations can't be done."

"Perhaps Wolfram and Hart have a spare Eye lying about."

"I wouldn't be surprised. But I wouldn't want to be the one trying to tune the collection either." Death magic amulets were notoriously finicky about interactions. Most of them were made, as a collection, from a single object, whether it was from a quarried rock or an enemy's bones. Trying to introduce one from a different source and persuade it to work properly with the others in a set was a large part of the reason that there were very few specialists in Sumerian death magic.

"Did you notice the books your friends from Wolfram and Hart are particularly interested in?" O'Flaherty remarked. "Odd for lawyers, don't you think?"

"Yes, I saw. Some of them may be considering changing careers. I can't say I'm particularly sympathetic."

"And here I thought you were the sympathetic sort." O'Flaherty didn't look at him as he said it. He didn't have to.

So you follow the dozen members of the sixth form down the Academy's paneled halls—not too far back, because you don't want to be accused of lagging, but far enough so you can see all of them. You think they must be mad to walk so quickly, almost trotting along the polished walnut floors.

Next to you, Madame Shearer, her head coming only to your shoulder, marches briskly, her heels tapping sharply against the ancient wood. Her blue eyes stare straight ahead.

"Mr. Stephens, Mr. O'Flaherty, Miss Leslye-Flindshym, turn left at the next corridor, if you please, and go through the double doors. We will then stop."

The little herd of teenagers enter as directed. It

*is not until they look at the stained-glass windows
above that they realize they have never been in this
particular room before.*

*You have been here, of course. Father brought you
here. As you watch the others' reactions, you realize
that one or two with parents high in the Council have
also been here before. The rest are much too curious
to comprehend where they truly are.*

*The room is circular and three stories high. A
catwalk encircles the third story, a low railing separating the walkway from the sheer drop. Above
the catwalk are the windows, sixteen of them. At
first glance they appear to be random shards of
color against hard lines of black.*

*Father said this is the Testing Room. More
Watchers have failed here than anywhere else.
When you asked him what kind of test, he snorted
and said, "Pray you never have to find out, boy."
Then he looked at you, consideringly, and said, "I
doubt you'll have to."*

*But here you are, despite everything, soon to
find out after all. You take a deep breath and
decide that you will pass this test, and he will be
proud. Even if everyone else in your class fails, you
will pass. Now if you can only understand what the
test will be. . . .*

"There's quite a nice little ceremonial bull's head
cup over on the third table. Lot seventy-six. I may

try for that," said O'Flaherty, looking at a set of scribbled notes. "I think it's original Sumerian. Do take a look at it, won't you? You'll be able to read the inscription better than I can."

Wesley had always taken top marks in Languages. He wasn't sure whether O'Flaherty was trying to be patronizing, but he drifted over to the indicated table, anyway.

The cup was, indeed, "quite nice." So "nice," it almost took his breath away: The arching bull's horns weren't gilt but solid gold, and the inscription—a dedication to Baal—was inlaid in clear, sky-blue Persian turquoise.

The raw materials alone were worth more than Wesley had budgeted for the next six months' living expenses.

"So? What do you think?"

With an acknowledging glance at the Tekhash demon standing beside the table, Wesley picked the cup up, ostensibly to take a closer look at the inscription, but in reality simply to feel the heft of the thing, the coolness of the gold against his hands. Even if one didn't consider its antiquity, and layers of power that made the cup almost vibrate against his fingertips, it was an object of exquisite beauty. The bull's eyes were obsidian glass, but somehow had a depth to them, as if it were watching him, deciding whether he was worthy.

Reluctantly, he put the cup back down. "Yes," he said. "Quite nice. I imagine it will go for a tidy sum."

"That's all right," O'Flaherty said casually, as if the prospect didn't dismay him in the least. He picked up a blown-glass Venetian spirit bottle and held it up to the sunlight, peering into the shifting mist inside as if he could determine the contents by sight alone.

"Are you bidding for yourself?" Wesley asked. "It's not the sort of thing one carries if one plans to travel light." Did O'Flaherty have the appropriate funds? Perhaps the man had managed to tap into one of the Watcher accounts.

While O'Flaherty sniffed at the rim of the stopper, the Tekhash guard approached as if afraid O'Flaherty was going to next try to open it. "Blast," O'Flaherty said as he placed the bottle back on the table. "Can't tell a thing with all these roses about. It could contain straight sewer gas, as far as I can tell."

With one more admiring glance at the ceremonial cup, Wesley returned to the area where he felt most comfortable, price-wise: the shabby cardboard boxes.

There was nothing here like the quality of the cup or the spirit bottle. Rummaging around, he came up with a lucky token from a Las Vegas casino, half a deck of Rider-Waite Tarot cards, and a battered rabbit's foot on a key chain. He tossed them back into the box and went on to the next one, only to find a paperback *Beginner's Tarot* with pages bookmarked by several of the major arcana missing from the Rider-Waite deck.

Trash, really. He wondered why Melchior's had even allowed this nonsense on the grounds.

The next box looked more promising—some older, odd-sized books with half-bound covers. He picked up one or two and glanced at the titles. Nothing he hadn't already read, unfortunately. Some of these he had memorized before he was even admitted to the Academy. Father's library had been extensive.

He dug further into the box, setting aside the top books. Lot ninety-four was really no different from any of the others on the table, but there was something about this box that just—caught at him.

His fingers tingled, almost the way they had in response to the Sumerian cup, as he dug deeper into the box's contents. Almost of themselves, they grasped hold of something near the bottom, and he pulled it out as if he had been blindly fishing for treasure in a child's game.

The volume in his hands was nearly black with age. If the cover had been cardboard, like that of modern books, it would have rotted away a lifetime ago; as it was, it was leather over real wooden boards, worn thin along the edge where who knew how many hands had held it. Looking closely at the seam where the spine was sewn, he could see traces of the original red dye that had colored the animal skin.

It might be a medieval book, based on the binding. It couldn't be much more recent, he thought. He'd have to have more time to examine it to be sure. It was possibly even a personal journal, a handmade book belonging to someone who had died centuries ago. Whatever it was, it practically *thrummed* in his hands.

He flipped open the front cover to take a quick look at the title page, taking the briefest glance at the words inscribed. As he did so, a loud chime rang. "Ladies and gentlemen, we are about to begin. Please prepare to take your seats."

He swallowed hard and made himself close the cover and drop the book back into the box. The other volumes he had looked at were still scattered over the table; he gathered them up hastily and put them on top.

"Something interesting?" O'Flaherty asked. "They're herding us toward the seats."

Wes picked up one of the books at random from the box and flipped through it. "Trash, mostly. Fred might like one or two of these." He dropped it back in and turned toward the chairs.

Lot ninety-four, he thought.

"If you're going to waste your money on that, I'll

be happy to go through them with you," O'Flaherty offered.

Giles would know if it was real, he told himself. And he might know more about O'Flaherty, too, and what he was really doing in Los Angeles, preparing to spend money like water.

But somehow he didn't want to share news of his possible—no, definite; he was absolutely going to buy that box of books, even if he had to burn everything else in it—acquisition with Giles. And besides, didn't he have reliable methods and sources of his own for obtaining information? He didn't need to go running to someone else, to share with someone else.

And speaking of reliable ways to unravel mysteries . . .

Wesley shrugged. "I might. But I thought you might be interested in something a little different this evening. Perhaps we'll go to Caritas," he said. "When was the last time you visited a demon bar for fun instead of mayhem?"

The auctioneer stepped up to the podium as they took their seats, among the last to do so. Wesley sat back and told himself to be patient as the long, late afternoon of bidding began.

CHAPTER SEVEN

It really was true, Adrian O'Flaherty decided; one could find anything in Los Angeles. In the thirties, it used to be Singapore, with its opium dens, grand British hotels, and spies everywhere. In the forties, fifties, and sixties, it was Berlin. Now it was Los Angeles, where you could walk into a bar and find a demon, with green skin and horns and bloodred eyes, singing jazz standards and Sinatra tunes. Old Red Eyes was doing Old Blue Eyes proud.

Caritas. Love? Someone's idea of a joke? He didn't think Pryce *had* a sense of humor. But the man must, to bring him here.

It took a moment to realize that the emcee was the same demon he'd been introduced to earlier at the Hyperion Hotel. Lorne, that was his name. Odd how a tux could change one's perception, even of a demon. He accepted a drink before realizing that the waitress also was a demon, and he barely managed to control his flinch.

Not well enough, apparently. Pryce was unable to hide his smirk.

"You have some very odd friends these days," O'Flaherty said. The drink was excellent, and he drank it far too quickly.

"One takes what one can get," Pryce answered. His hand rose involuntarily, as if to rub at the fearsome scar on his neck. When he saw O'Flaherty staring, he dropped his hand quickly to his glass. Questions were clearly not going to be welcome. "Lorne came here from the Pylea dimension because he didn't fit in among his own kind. And, they didn't have music."

"That would have been a waste."

It was quite amazing, the variety of songs the demon knew. His repertoire was by no means limited to the pop tunes of the forties and fifties, although those seemed to be his favorites; in the forty-five minutes or so that they watched and listened, he also included a medley of Irish drinking songs, German lieder, and sixties rock 'n' roll. And he made it work, too, although belting out "Smoke Gets in Your Eyes" was much more his style.

"All right, my little songbirds and songbird-ettes," announced Lorne onstage. "Time for me to take a little breaky-poo, and then it's your turn.

Drinks are half-price during the interlude—build up the old Dutch courage."

There was scattered applause as the house lights came up. It was much easier now to see the variety of people—and non-people—seated at the round tables and at the bar. A table seating six Japanese businessmen was next to another with a pair of Umlok demons, and the two tables were exchanging cards, complete with social bows. The Umloks couldn't bow back—they didn't have flexible spines—but they were snorting gentle puffs of steam as a return courtesy.

At another table, an elderly man and an elegantly attired woman held hands, while a vampire in full fang face leered over their shoulders.

Flight attendants still in uniform were chatting with Hebbetskek demons, trading packing tips, as near as O'Flaherty could tell. He wondered how a Hebbetskek could get past airport security in this day and age. Did they have to check those razor-sharp horns at the X-ray machine? Or did they just impale the security people and waltz on through?

"How on earth can this place exist?" O'Flaherty asked. "We ought to stake at least three of those vampires by the door before they start snacking on the audience. There are demons in here who are natural enemies, and yet humans who sit here as if—including *us*, I might point out—!"

"Anti-violence spell," Pryce answered. He was

watching Lorne, who had paused beside a table of Wolfram & Hart lawyers—at least O'Flaherty *assumed* they were from Wolfram & Hart; he recognized two of them from the auction, though the third was a stunning brunette—or was her hair auburn? It was difficult to tell, in this light. She looked over and saw the two of them, and lifted her glass in salute. "A really excellent anti-violence spell."

Not to "them," O'Flaherty realized. To Pryce. Who nodded back, coolly.

Well, well, well. How interesting. "Who is she?"

"Lilah Morgan. Rather senior—head of their Special Projects group. Interesting to see her here."

"She appears to know you."

"She thinks she does."

O'Flaherty glanced at him, startled at the restrained venom in the words, only to find Pryce's gaze on him now. *I wonder if he suspects*, he thought. *I wonder if I should tell him. Perhaps he could help. . . .*

But then: *No. This is* my *business. No one else's. Certainly not Prig Pryce's.*

He settled back in his chair, prepared to enjoy more of the show, when he saw, not Lorne, but a wispy-looking girl in her early twenties stumble onto the stage, holding the microphone as if it were an ice-cream cone.

"All right, girls and boys! Are we feeling the love here tonight?" yelled Lorne, now seated in the audience. Horror of horrors, it was karaoke time. "Let's hear it for Donna! Come on, Donna! Sing it for us!"

He shot a disbelieving look at Pryce, who was genuinely smiling now, as if he actually enjoyed watching this poor child make an utter fool of herself. The music swelled, and she tried to find a note—any note. The music hastily changed keys and tune to match her rendition of "Moon River." Donna left no note unflattened in her march through the verses. Pryce was watching with evident pleasure. The man had untapped depths of sadism.

O'Flaherty swiveled his head to see if Lorne, who—demon or not—had demonstrated clear musical taste, could tolerate the travesty on the stage. But the green demon was watching Donna intently, as if the woman's every breath was a lesson in stagecraft.

Finally, mercifully, she wound down, and he joined everyone else in frantic applause. "Let's hear it for Donna, folks!" said Lorne. "Wasn't that a brave performance?" It certainly was *brave*, if not exactly a performance. Lorne went up to escort her back to her table. "All right, who's going to be next tonight?"

There was a certain amount of scrambling as

several people vied to be next up on the stage. Finally, a demon was selected to yowl and grunt through a country-western song. O'Flaherty was beginning to think that nothing would surprise him in this place anymore.

Then Ms. Morgan leaned over and tapped the arm of one of the men from Wolfram & Hart. He jumped, and turned to stare at her, shocked. She jerked her head at the stage, clearly telling him to get up there and sing, and just as clearly, he didn't want to.

Not that he had any choice—that is, until Lorne put one hand on his shoulder and moved him back into his chair, saying something cheerful to the woman as he did so. She didn't like it, whatever it was. Her response was one of those brittle smiles that he thought of as a "cocktail smile," as false as cheap gin. The man at the table looked both relieved and upset, as if making Lilah Morgan angry wasn't worth not going onstage.

"What's that all about?" he asked Pryce, nodding at the little byplay.

Pryce hiked an eyebrow. "Looks like Lorne doesn't want to hear from Lilah's little friend. Maybe he thinks she won't get anything out of the performance and doesn't want her to waste her time." He seemed to think it was funny.

Now Lorne had left the table and was offering the microphone to various members of the audience, letting them sing a few lines of song between banter. Once, he put his hand on a man's face and sang to him, a soft, lonely song O'Flaherty had never heard before and wasn't sure he ever wanted to hear again; it reminded him too much of why he was here, of unfinished business. The man broke down in sobs.

No one in the audience seemed surprised.

The demon waitress set a new glass down in front of him. This was what, the third? Fourth? He had lost count; she kept taking the empties away, and he was certain he wasn't paying. He was also certain Pryce wasn't drinking as much as he was.

He shouldn't be drinking. He was drinking too much, a stupid, stupid thing for a Watcher to be doing. Watchers were supposed to kill monsters. Demons. Not drink in demon bars. But he wasn't a Watcher anymore. There weren't any Watchers.

"What are you planning to do with all the books you bought today?" Pryce asked casually. "And that mask. Good lord, that thing is massive."

"What?"

"From the auction. For someone traveling light, that was quite a haul."

The auction. Yes. He took a deep breath and decided he wasn't as drunk as he'd like to think he was. Certainly nowhere near as drunk as Pryce would like to think he was. He could always drink the Prig under the table, anyway. "I thought I might send them home," he said. "We lost the library. But it's still needed, you know. Even if we aren't."

Pryce was looking puzzled. "We aren't? Oh, you mean the Watchers. Well, not specifically, perhaps. But in general"—he made a small gesture with his head, taking in the whole audience of demons, vampires, humans—"I would say that people trained as we were are probably going to be needed, still, for a good long time." He looked over at the Wolfram & Hart table and let open envy show in his voice for just a moment. "It's hard luck that they got that Healy translation at the auction. If anyone has a collection to rival what ours was, they do. They'll do anything to get what they want." The venom wasn't as well disguised now. "Anything."

Perhaps Pryce wasn't entirely sober after all.

And here was Lorne, two tables away, holding out his microphone to a woman and urging her to sing. And listening to her so intently. Watching her with those bloody demon eyes, as if drinking her up, as if he was feeding off the music, gaining some kind of unholy sustenance from it—

It hit him like a shock, sobering him abruptly, and it was all he could do to remain still. The demon listened to the woman sing three lines from a song and then leaned over, put that comforting hand on her arm, and spoke to her in a soothing voice, confidentially, so that no one could hear but herself.

And she listened to him, smiled, and nodded. Just as the others had, most of them. These people volunteered to sing for this bastard. They *came here* to sing for him. They *knew* what he was doing.

Because he was giving something back to them.

Twenty years of Watcher discipline kept him from swearing aloud.

This was Wesley Wyndam-Pryce's colleague at Angel Investigations. He was a demon, and he was a bloody empath who picked up something from people's minds when they sang.

"Well! Look who's here! Our old friend Wes and his buddy—Adrian O'Flaherty, isn't that the name? How about giving us a couple of bars of an English pub song, Adrian?"

He was in the process of swallowing, anyway; it wasn't hard to inhale just at the wrong time as well. The liquor obediently went down the wrong pipe, and he doubled over, choking, coughing, to get it clear.

"Oh, dear! That sounds bad! Wes, give the man some water." O'Flaherty took an offered sip but waved Lorne off. The coughing went on for some time, and he was appropriately red in the face by the time he was able to straighten up and breathe normally.

"Not this evening, I'm afraid," he croaked out.

"Too bad, we would have loved to hear from you. Maybe next time."

Lorne moved on.

It was time to go home. Watchers were supposed to kill demons, not drink in demon bars.

Even if he wasn't a Watcher anymore.

And even if he wasn't looking for a demon to kill anymore, but a man.

Emilio was in his room, trying to read one of the books he'd taken from Cawber's, when he heard the old Buick pull into the driveway. He thought about going to the window to check, but he knew the sound of his father's car. His dad liked to pretend it was a classic car, but a 1976 two-door? No way. And his leg *hurt* where the little demon had sunk its claws in this afternoon.

He pulled up the leg of his jeans to look. At least he *could* pull them up this time—for a while, his leg had been too swollen. He couldn't even bend it. Now the swelling was going down, but the rips across his skin were still obvious. And there were ugly green streaks going up and down his leg, and it was really hot. He wondered about rabies. Did demons get rabies?

He couldn't concentrate. He put the book aside, along with all the others spread out over his bed, and lay back on the pillows, staring up at the Britney Spears poster on his ceiling. Britney would feel sorry for him and his hurt leg, he thought resentfully. Not like his mom and his sister, who didn't even notice him come in.

He could hear his father saying hello to his mother—he always made such a big deal out of that—and then, like he always did, he went into his office. He never stopped working. You'd think he could afford better stuff than that whale of a 1976 Buick, with its dorky headlights and wanna-be fins and a trunk you could put two weeks' worth of groceries in and still have room to sleep six, as his mom said—if you tied the lid down first.

He was surprised by the knock at his door.

"Emilio?"

He was even more surprised to hear his father's voice. He sat up quickly, caught his breath at a wave of dizziness, and was just able to shove his jeans leg back down before the bedroom door opened.

"Emilio? Your mother says the school called. You haven't been going to classes." His father came into his room—didn't he know anything about privacy?—and stood over him. He sounded sad.

Emilio knew better than to look up. The old man might *sound* sad, but he was really ticked off. And he was close enough to hit him. He also knew better than to say anything.

"What are you doing in here by yourself? You should be out there with the rest of the family."

Yeah, right. Like *he* ever spent time with the rest of the family.

"What are all these books?"

Emilio looked up at that, just in time to see his father lean over and pick up the book he'd been reading. He tried to pull it out of his father's hands. That was a mistake. He found himself sprawling back on the bed as the result of a casual slap.

"Don't you try to take things away from me," his father said. "I feed you, I clothe you, I put a roof over your head, and everything you've *got* belongs to me. And don't you forget it." He skimmed through the book, grunted in surprise, and reached for the others. "What the hell have you got here? This looks like stuff from the library at work. How'd you get these?"

The library at *work*? What kind of legal library would have this stuff? "I got them at a store," Emilio said, passing the back of his hand over his mouth. His face stung where his father had connected.

"Don't tell me that. These look valuable. I'm going to take them in and have Dr. Circe appraise them. They're not the kind of thing a kid should have."

"They're mine!" Emilio protested.

His father raised his head and stared at him over the open book. "Yours? Didn't you hear what I just told you? There is no 'yours.' Even if you *did* buy them, which I doubt, you did so with money you got from me. So don't tell me 'yours.'" He piled up the books in his arms and turned for the door. "Don't let me catch you with this kind of thing again, you hear me? Or we'll have ourselves a little discussion about what's yours, and following orders. Now get on out there and join your mother and sister."

Emilio watched him go, helpless rage bubbling up. He didn't move from the bed; his father would go directly to his office—do not stop, do not pass go—and he'd be there for the rest of the evening. He always did.

His father was going to take his books in to work? Who was Dr. Circe, and what did *he* know about this stuff? Could he be the guy in the park this afternoon?

If he was, Emilio decided, he really, really wanted to meet this dude. Maybe he'd be like Cawber, and be more understanding about stuff than his dad was.

Anybody had to be more understanding than his dad was.

He smiled bitterly, thinking about the little red demons, imagining them swarming over his father. His father wouldn't give him static about what was his when *that* happened, he bet.

Angel tapped impatiently on the counter as he listened to Wes's report. "No kids at the auction."

"No kids," Wes confirmed. His voice was staticky

over the cell phone, and Angel wished that the other man was reporting in person rather than from his home. Sometimes this business of trying to get things back to where they were was impossible. Things could never be the way they used to be.

"And I didn't see anyone who might be buying for a teenager, either," Wesley continued through the static. "Although there were several of the owners of the smaller occult shops. None of them purchased anything of note, as far as I could see, however."

"Hmph." The pencil stuttered out a staccato slip jig rhythm from the early days, before his death, before he rose again as a vampire. He caught himself at it and laid the pencil down. "What about your Watcher buddy?"

"Now that was rather interesting," Wesley admitted. "I'm not certain where he got the funds—perhaps he's accessed some of the Watcher accounts—but he had quite a lot of money, and spent it rather freely."

"Patterns?"

"Not that I could determine." Wesley sounded rather annoyed by that. "Some standard history texts—things I would have expected him to have already, but I suppose they would have been lost when the library was destroyed. And a few really esoteric things. One or two I would have liked myself." Pure jealousy flickered for just a moment

in the civilized, even tones, and was promptly
smothered. Angel grinned. "Several rather interesting artifacts, among them a gold Sumerian cup
and lyre, and a Kwandishet spell mask."

"What? That's huge. That's probably bigger than
he is. What's he planning to do, carry it around
with him?"

"I believe he's planning on shipping it home,
along with his other purchases."

"So he still has a base of operations."

"Either that, or he was telling the truth about
trying to help re-create the Watcher collection."

Angel thought about that. "Not our business, if he
is," he decided. "I'm more worried about what he's
doing here, not back there. What did Lorne say?"

Now Wes was making no attempt to disguise his
disgust. "Lorne didn't have a chance to read him.
O'Flaherty figured out what he was doing and
managed to avoid singing for him."

"Aye, and he's a canny son of Erin, isn't he?"
Angel couldn't decide whether he was as annoyed
as Wesley was, or proud of a fellow countryman
even if the fellowship dated back a few centuries.
On the whole, annoyance predominated, but there
was something about being Irish that never quite
went away, even when you were centuries dead
and hanging out in L.A.

"Indeed." Wesley's reaction was English to the
core.

Angel managed to cover up a snicker. The Kingdom might call itself United, but the English and the Irish would always regard each other as separate. "Anything else?"

A pause from the other end. "Wolfram and Hart seemed particularly interested in spells of accountancy. I wonder whether they might not be having some problems with the demons who run the Internal Revenue Service."

Angel laughed out loud. "Couldn't happen to a nicer bunch of people."

"How is Charles recovering from his injuries?" Wes asked, changing the subject. "Is the new batch of ointment acceptable?"

"Yeah, doing the job just fine. He'll be back on the streets tomorrow."

"Tonight," Gunn said from across the room.

"Tomorrow," Angel said firmly.

"I see he's fully recovered," Wes remarked. "Very well. I'm going to call it a night myself. I'll be in touch."

"Good. And thanks, Wes. I appreciate your looking into this for me."

"No problem." The connection cut off.

Angel stared at the cell phone thoughtfully before putting it down on the counter.

"So do we know any more about our kiddy wiz problem?" Gunn asked. He and Angel were the only ones in the hotel at the moment; Cordelia and

Fred had gone to a drugstore down the street on an errand of their own.

"Not a thing."

"Did we really think we were going to?"

Angel shrugged. "I had hopes."

"Maybe this last vision was it. And it's over."

"Maybe," Angel said. "But I don't think so."

Wesley set the cell phone on the arm of the chair and stared at the cardboard box resting on the coffee table in front of him. He could wait until morning to go through it. That might be more reasonable. If he started tonight, there was a very good chance he would never get to bed at all. If he went to bed, he could tackle the box in the morning, refreshed and rested.

A snort of amusement escaped him. He wouldn't sleep; he'd lie awake most of the night, wondering. Wondering whether he'd allowed himself to be deluded by a chance resemblance to a half-remembered description, or whether he really did have something rare and wonderful in a box of what was otherwise complete junk.

He went into the kitchen and found the bottle of whiskey from which he'd poured O'Flaherty's drink two nights before. No ginger ale this evening, thank you. He measured a careful two fingers, and then added a reckless splash before returning to his chair. He set the drink aside and pulled the box onto the floor in front of him.

The now-sealed box opened without difficulty. Inside, the auctioneer's receipt for payment lay on top of a jumble of books and pamphlets. He made himself take them out one by one and examine each individually, piling them neatly on the coffee table in stacks according to size or subject. *Your Love Horoscope. 30,000 Ways to Beat the Casinos. Your Lucky Numbers. Love Spells.* A collection of old horror novels by people he had never heard of. TV gossip magazines dating back to the 1970s. Hardback books in various states of disrepair: some boards cracked, water stained, dust covers ripped when they were present at all. Someone must have been cleaning out his basement.

For a moment he panicked. Had he been imagining things? Was this garbage all there was? Had he spent good coin on *this*? Surely he had seen, had actually held in his hands—

Yes. He could tell as soon as his fingers closed on it. It felt *different*. Was the tingle in his fingertips his imagination as they touched the worn leather of the binding? It was a much older book than the others in the box. Of course it would feel different. He pulled it out from under a layer of magazines and tourist pamphlets, where he had earlier hid it from casual view. Here was the true reason he had bid on Lot ninety-four.

The leather was dry and crumbling under his

reverential fingers, and he had to look closely to be able to tell that it was originally dyed crimson; untold years of handling, unknown numbers of hands had blackened it. He had first been attracted to its antiquity, as a magpie would be attracted to something shiny, and when his hands had felt the weight of the book, he'd had to flip it open and look at the title page.

And then he had known that he had to own it, no matter what the cost.

He held his prize, weighing it in his palms: *A Compendium of auntient Graymarye after the teachings of another, and a Treatise wherein Essays tending to the Advancement of Learning of such not Commonly Used, on the Authoritie of various of the Wise; and an Anatomie of Abuses to be avoided.*

They were much given, those Jacobeans, to excessively lengthy titles. "That was before," Madame Shearer had observed, "the invention of the synopsis." He smiled at the memory.

Everyone else called it the Red Compendium.

"What's that, Father?"

His father stared at him over the top of his glasses and snorted. "Nothing for you to be concerned with, boy. Far beyond your comprehension."

If it *was* the actual Red Compendium—the book that other books referred to, always obliquely—it was supposed to be an ultimate collection of the great spells "after the teachings of another." But who the "another" was, was never quite specified. The Abuses to be Avoided, of course, were always cataloged at length and with great imagination. None of the great sorcerers or magicians ever openly admitted reading or contributing to the Compendium, but some of them let it be rumored that their work was incorporated into it. It was considered the height of bad taste to actually ask anyone point-blank.

And now here he was, Wesley Wyndam-Pryce, ex-Watcher, rogue demon hunter, sitting in an apartment in Los Angeles, California, with a glass of rather good whiskey at his feet and the very book itself balanced in his hands. He wondered what O'Flaherty would have said if he had known. He'd have thrown over that Kwandishet spell mask in a heartbeat; he'd have given a dozen gold Sumerian cups to have half an hour with this book.

And he *owned* it. If this really was the Compendium, it was worth all the other books of spells that had been on offer in the auction. And it had been buried among the trash in a box of odd lots.

It was so unlikely, he was certain he was fooling himself. He put the book down, wiped his hands on his thighs, and took a long draft of the whiskey, trying to restore a sense of reality to the situation. It had to be someone's idea of a joke.

Someone had read about the Compendium somewhere and had made up a dummy, created an old leather binding, printed up a convincing-looking title page, and planted it in the auction. There were probably a dozen copies exactly like this one in a dozen boxes being opened tonight all over the city.

He took another swallow of his drink, coughed, and blinked as the fumes tickled his sinuses. Well, he did have to give them credit. It was a very convincing fake. It wasn't quite the right dimensions as a modern book. And that was real leather in the binding, he would swear to that—it smelled right, and it felt right too.

If it was a joke, a forgery, it was an artistic one. He could at least give the forger the courtesy of examining his work.

Besides, his glass was empty.

He picked the book up again, hefted it, and carefully opened the front cover. For a book as old as this one purported to be, it was certainly well sewn; all the pages were tight, none falling out. As if the book were loath to let them go.

And the title page with its ridiculously long, elaborate title.

He turned the page.

Despite himself, he began to read.

And he fell into the book.

CHAPTER EIGHT

The Los Angeles office of Wolfram & Hart was a modern building, unlike the London branch's. The London branch's office dated to just after the Great Fire (naturally, since the company had considerable to do with setting it), and the place overlooked the parks and greenery of the inner city.

It had once been a private residence, the property of an Earl. He and his Countess and their two daughters—and the forty-nine members of domestic staff required to keep His Lordship's family in minimal comfort—had occupied the building that would have covered an entire New York City block. The facade survived the fire, but its original golden glow, quarried from Cornish stone pits, had been charred black. Centuries of coal fires and city smog only reinforced its image.

The city appealed to the firm to join the restoration effort that was sprucing up the British Museum,

the Royal Library, even Westminister Abbey. But
the firm loftily ignored all such requests. The stone
of the London branch, protected by spells, would
never soften and crumble under the attack of acids
and bacteria in the dark patina. And they rather liked
being The Black Building.

The Watchers Council had long had moles
within the London branch of Wolfram & Hart.
Adrian O'Flaherty had been one of them, in his
many undercover jobs for the Council as they
sought information about one of the most evil cor-
porations in the world. He was fairly confident that
his cover had never been broken, and the disguise
spells he had used had never been penetrated.

The upstart, New World Los Angeles office was
far more modern, and featured glass and concrete
towers. It looked, in fact, like any downtown office
building occupied by a successful law firm, broker-
age, or insurance company. When Adrian O'Flaherty stepped through the glass doors into the
air-conditioned lobby, early in the afternoon of the
day after the auction, the receptionist at the information desk nodded to him pleasantly. The men
and woman crossing back and forth between banks
of elevators, briefcases and file folders tucked
under their arms, all looked perfectly normal and
reassuringly businesslike, like associates and junior
partners busy working on wills and trusts and corporate buyouts.

But how many of them worked in divisions such as Ritual Sacrifice, Demonic Alliances, and Special Projects? Wolfram & Hart even managed to give their Real Estate Division their own special spin.

"May I help you, sir?" The receptionist was professional, cool, and self-possessed. He could see her assessing him: Who was he, was he dangerous?

He smiled engagingly and slipped her a business card. "Here to see Ms. Lilah Morgan."

She blinked at the name, and one perfectly manicured hand reached out to press a button on the keyboard in front of her. Then she glanced down at the card, and paled. "Could you wait just one moment, please, Mr., er, O'Flaherty?"

"Certainly, darling." He leaned over, resting his forearms on the desk. "She isn't expecting me," he confided, watching her type frantically. He caught a glimpse of the words "Watchers Council" before the encryption software snatched it out of comprehension.

She looked up at him and tried to jerk the monitor out of his range of vision. "Sir, if you don't mind—"

"Oh, not in the least." He smiled again and stepped back, just as a security guard came up behind him.

"Is there a problem here, Lorelei?" the guard asked.

"No," she quavered, studying her screen. A

discreet buzzer sounded, and she said, "Yes? Yes, ma'am. Of course, ma'am, right away. With an escort? Jacobsen is right here. Yes, ma'am."

She swallowed hard and looked up at the guard. "Please show Mr. O'Flaherty up to Ms. Morgan's office." She turned back to O'Flaherty. "I—I hope you don't mind the delay. She says she's very much looking forward to meeting you, sir."

"And the feeling is absolutely mutual, darling." He grinned at her again, blew her a kiss, turned to Jacobsen, and gestured to the brown-uniformed guard to lead on.

O'Flaherty had always felt that one could best judge the real quality of a business by the state of its elevators. The executive elevators at Wolfram & Hart were very high quality indeed—real wood paneling, highly polished brass railings without a hint of tarnish, carpet so thick, it was like standing on a cloud. It moved silently, not even a purr of power, only the change of air pressure and the weight of his own body as they rose told him they were moving.

Jacobsen wasn't used to such rarified heights, O'Flaherty observed. The guard was becoming more and more uneasy as they got closer and closer to the upper floors. He pulled a card from his wallet and checked it repeatedly.

The elevator stopped, and the doors slid open to reveal a carpeted hallway. The guard took one more look at his card and slid it back into the wallet. "This way."

O'Flaherty followed, one eyebrow arched. He might rate an escort, but not an experienced one, obviously.

Jacobsen was not only inexperienced, he was also very grateful to leave O'Flaherty with Lilah Morgan's secretary and disappear back down the hallway. O'Flaherty was left to occupy a chair for another twenty minutes before a door opened and the woman he had seen the night before at Caritas welcomed him into her office.

"Mr. O'Flaherty, is it? This is a rare pleasure. It isn't often that we're able to welcome a Watcher to our offices."

He indulged himself for a moment or two. She was worth the time to look at. Despite the perfectly proper dark blue business skirt and jacket, she managed to exude sex appeal. The skirt was long enough to be appropriate and short enough to notch his blood pressure upward; the double-zipped blazer showed the clean lines of her throat and hinted at more. Her lips were pursed ever so slightly as she watched him watching her. From across the room, he could sense, rather than scent, her perfume.

Looking forward to meeting him, was she? The waiting game was so much nonsense, and she would know he knew it. He stifled a smirk, looked around, chose a chair, and sat down without an invitation. She smiled and leaned back against the polished mahogany table, crossing trim ankles.

"Your record remains inviolate, I'm afraid," he said. "There are no more Watchers. So I'm not here as one. I'm afraid I haven't had time to update the card."

"Ah." It was the perfect noncommittal response, neither agreeing nor disagreeing. "Well, Mr. O'Flaherty who is no longer a Watcher, what can Wolfram and Hart do for you?"

He crossed his legs and laced his fingers over his knee. "I noticed that you had representatives at the Gilman auction yesterday. Your organization has always had quite a reputation, one might almost say a talent, for acquiring interesting items."

"Why, Mr. O'Flaherty, you flatter us. Dare I hope you might be looking for a position that gives you access to some of those items?"

He hesitated, considering. "I wasn't aware such a position was available, Ms. Morgan."

"Oh, call me Lilah."

He smiled.

"A position is always available to a man with talent."

"I would hate to displace someone with talent," he parried. "Don't you already have, I don't know, a librarian or curator or head of research or something?"

"Or something," she agreed. "So if you're not look-ing for a job, Mr. O'Flaherty, what are you looking for? I have to warn you, we're not in the habit of loan-ing out our acquisitions, if that's what you're after."

That would be as good an excuse as anything, he decided, since she clearly wasn't going to give him a direct answer to the question he knew better than to ask directly. "That's such a pity," he said, and sighed. "You're certain you never de-access anything? Because you're aware of our losses, of course. I was hoping that you'd allow us to pick up whatever discards you might have."

She stared at him a moment. "You're not seri-ous."

"Why not?"

"You do recall that we're on opposite sides of the whole Good-Evil thing? You're Good, I'm Evil? And you want our leftovers? You've got to be kid-ding!"

"Beggars can't be choosers."

"Why should we help you by even that much?"

He gave it some thought, lifted his brows. "Amusement factor?"

She laughed. "I think I've gotten enough amuse-ment just out of this meeting, Mr. O'Flaherty," she said. "For a man who's no longer a Watcher, you throw around the term 'us' pretty easily. Could it be that the Council isn't quite as dead as you'd like me to believe?"

For an instant the memory of the Council Library, a collapsed, smoking ruin, flashed through his mind. "No," he said roughly. He took a deep breath and got his voice, if not his feelings, back under control. "No, the Council is dead. Those few of us who remain aren't organized. Whoever did this to us was very thorough."

"You have to admire good workmanship," Lilah said lightly. "And if you're wondering, as far as I know, no, it wasn't us. We prefer more indirect methods of dealing with our . . . adversaries."

"I wasn't intending to accuse you." And he wasn't; he was satisfied that Wolfram & Hart had had nothing to do with the Council disaster. This particular blow had come from a different direction.

And he wasn't here to avenge the Council, in any case. They could take care of their own, as he would take care of his. "And I wasn't looking for employment. Though I do appreciate the offer."

"That offer still stands, at least for the time being. You know how to get in touch." She paused, waiting for him to speak. When he said nothing, she continued, "But if you'll excuse me, I have innocents to debauch and lives to destroy, and all of that sort of thing."

"Of course, Ms. Morgan. Thank you for your time." He rose, and took the hand she offered. She wore no rings. Her nails were short and glossy. Her hand was cool and strong.

"Lilah, please, Mr. O'Flaherty."

He merely smiled, and nodded, and waited for her to call for someone to escort him out of the building. The shivers she produced—well, it might be repulsion, but it was, he admitted to himself, probably something else entirely.

He waited until he was out of the building to relax.

"Well," said Lilah Morgan, "wasn't *that* a perfectly useless meeting." She circled the desk and sat down, swiveling back and forth in frustration. She didn't believe for a moment that he had walked in to talk to her about artifacts. He wanted something, and when a man wanted something, he was vulnerable. There had to be a way to get to the guy; you didn't let a former Watcher just slip away.

At least, not *another* former Watcher.

Come to think of it, there must be at least a few more former Watchers still out there, mustn't there? All the ones who weren't killed off before the Big Bang, and whoever had survived it. "All those talented people without a purpose left in life," she mused. "I'll bet we could find them a purpose if we really tried."

She made a note to work up a proposal for the senior partners. Now, who could she get to take the risk of broaching the idea who wouldn't take actual credit for it if they turned out to love it?

She was mentally running through the latest list of new associates when the interoffice link buzzed.

"Dr. Circe, Ms. Morgan. Line two."

Circe? What did *he* want? Speaking of leftover artifacts and de-accessing—

"Rutherford? What a pleasant surprise. What can I do for you?" She was careful to keep her voice pleasant and noncommittal. She might be Head of Special Projects, but Rutherford Circe was the Librarian. He might not have power in the table of organization sense, but he had access to more *information* than almost anyone in the company. Even the psychics reported to him.

"You can flay those bloody incompetent minions of yours alive, for starters."

She blinked. "Well, that's certainly an option, Rutherford. Would you care to tell me why?" He was such a disagreeable man. What a pity O'Flaherty wouldn't take the bait. She was certain he'd be so much more pleasant to deal with. Employee relations were important.

"I sent them to that auction with specific instructions to find the rarest, most precious books and artifacts. I have spent years looking for some of these items."

Years. She wondered what Circe would make of the suggestion that he clean out the Library and turn over some of his "precious books and artifacts" to the remains of the Watchers Council.

He'd probably have a fit. The man had no sense of irony at all.

"And what's the problem, Rutherford? I know they spent quite a lot. I countersigned the vouchers myself. Are you saying they didn't deliver what I signed for?" Perhaps flaying *wasn't* an unreasonable response. The company took a dim view of spending corporate funds for personal use. Even though it had a flexible definition of "personal use."

The voice at the other end of the line practically spat venom. "Oh, of course they delivered the purchases. All of them were logged into the Library by noon today. There's no problem there.

"The problem is that the fools failed to review the random assessment of the job lots."

"Excuse me, Rutherford?" If the stuff they'd paid for had been delivered, what was he so upset about? And why was he bothering *her* about it?

The cultivated voice was bitter and clipped. "I've just gone through the catalog. In the back of the catalog is a listing of the job lots, with a random list of their contents. The random list ensures that the contents of the job lot fits in with the auction. It also allows buyers to locate lots in which they might be interested. Generally, the job lots at an auction of this sort consist of . . . junk."

Lengthy explanations could be annoying. Lilah examined the straps of her Manolo Blahniks.

Scuffs? Surely not. "If it's junk, Rutherford, what's the problem?"

And if he didn't get that patronizing tone out of his voice, employee relations be damned, Wolfram & Hart would be looking for a new Librarian.

"Because occasionally it is *not* junk, Ms. Morgan. And in this case, I find, listed very clearly on page one hundred and seventy-six of the catalog, column three, Lot ninety-four: 'Assorted Books, Including: *Tarot Divination, Las Vegas Card Reading,* and"—his voice dropped—"*A Compendium of auntient Graymarye after the teachings of another.*'"

She checked her manicure. "And this is important, I gather?" Still unchipped. Nice little spell, that.

"The Red Compendium, Ms. Morgan." Not only patronizing, but impatient, too. "If this is the actual *Compendium of auntient Graymarye*, it's the most extensive collection of spells ever collected. It's an amazing opportunity. And your associates let it slip through their fingers!"

She would have let it slip through *her* fingers too, but she wasn't going to tell Rutherford Circe that. And if he'd just found it in the catalog, it sounded like he had been the one to slip up. "Was this something you had asked them to look for specifically, Rutherford? Were they alerted to expect it?"

"They were alerted. Your Mr. Herrera said, and I quote, 'It wasn't auctioned, Mr. Circe. It must have been withdrawn or sold privately ahead of time.' As if Melchior's do private sales! They simply didn't bother to check. And we've lost it."

She could sympathize with his frustration. Up to a point. She wondered whether the alert her people had gotten was before or after the fact. After, she was willing to bet. Her associates knew better than to ignore specific instructions, and that catalog description Circe had quoted was very specific. "What category of spells are we talking about, then? Summoning? Exorcising? Killing? Cursing?"

A windy sigh came through the phone, and she pulled the receiver away from her ear in distaste.

"All of that and more," he said. "The Compendium isn't a collection of a single type of spell. From what I've been able to determine, it's truly a random collection of some of the most powerful spells of some of the most powerful sorcerers ever known—spells of cursing, spells of healing, of summoning and banishing. The only characteristic they have in common is that they all seem to have been the last spells of the sorcerers and magicians who crafted them. It would have been an invaluable addition to our collection."

"It does sound like it." Perhaps it was a good thing Lorne had refused to let that little twerp Herrera sing last night after all. She'd wanted to know what Circe had asked him to do; well, now she knew. That was always assuming Circe was telling the truth about the briefing, and she already didn't believe him about that. But if the man had sung for Lorne, then the empathic Pylean would have picked up on something related to this Compendium, and probably run right off to tell Wesley about it. "Let me think about this for a minute, Circe."

As it was, the twerp had another future laid out for him now, and the Pylean would have seen that as well. And it was such an annoyance when junior associates tried to save their own skins. Had Linwood Murrow, the former Special Representative of the senior partners, whom she had killed to take her present exalted position, allowed *her* such leeway to think for herself?

Well, no. But she'd taken it anyway, and that's how she'd gotten the corner office.

All right. She could see a way to turn this into a win. Circe was out for blood; well, she could accommodate him. It wasn't as if the twerp was a rising star or anything like that. This way she could hire somebody to replace him, somebody who didn't get calls in the middle of the day from his wife about kids at school.

That should pacify Circe until she could find out who had actually bought this Lot ninety-four. Although she still didn't see what the big deal was;

surely everything in this book had to already be in the Library.

That would teach her not to waste money taking associates out for a drink the next time, though. If Circe was so eager to get the book that he just called her up and told her all about it, well, eager people made mistakes, and Lilah was good at capitalizing on other people's mistakes.

She was taking too long to "think about this." Even though she'd known immediately what to do, Circe would think she wasn't fast on her feet.

On the other hand, was that a bad thing? Let him. His mistake!

She had a feeling her earlier visitor wouldn't be that stupid. She'd known he was sharp when she'd seen him last night. Pity about the company he kept.

Last night—that reminded her yet again of seeing Wesley, and she was determined *not* to think about Wesley Wyndam-Pryce.

At least, not until she had a way to get him back on her side. Or at least back in her bed.

She took a deep breath. "All right, Rutherford. I can certainly see your point, and appropriate discipline is called for. We can't have this kind of carelessness. I'll send Herrera right over, and of course the others who had this assignment. However, I'd very much appreciate it if you'd conserve the blood. I was going over the quarterly sacrifice budget this morning, and it will be a big help." Not that she really needed the help, but it was always a good idea to let them think you owed them a favor.

"I'd be glad to," he said, somewhat mollified. "Thank you, Ms. Morgan."

She snorted silently. Having put the idea in his head, she'd be surprised to see even half of the stuff show up in her accounts. The Library would take most of it.

"Of course I'll do everything I can to trace the purchaser of that particular lot—ninety-four, I believe you said?—and we'll retrieve the book immediately." Of course she would. But she'd have her own people look at it carefully before turning it over to the Library. There had to be some reason Circe was so eager for it.

"That's very kind of you." Now that his anger had been vented, Circe was almost ingenuous in his enthusiasm. "If this really is the actual book, I've heard that it may have the Danetti restoration spell. Our files are sadly lacking in that area. It would be wonderful to be able to add a mental restoration spell to the file."

Lilah, busy taking notes of people she wanted to send over to the Library, paused in mid-scribble. "A mental restoration spell?"

"Oh, yes. Reputed to return the mad, the senile, the grieving, the tortured to complete mental acuity. Really quite amazing."

She swallowed. "This sort of thing isn't particularly

in our line of work. It's a temporary restoration, I assume?"

"Oh, no. A permanent return. It was Danetti's crowning achievement. His notes were quite extensive, and they indicate that he carried it out successfully at least twice. I'm certain that we can find a way to use it on individuals, for example, who seek to escape questioning through madness. Or even to retrieve information from some older sorcerers who have fallen victim to dementia.

"But of course the most exciting applications are in the area of spell reversal. With the complete spell in hand, we should be able to select the victim of our choice and drive him or her mad. And depending on the variables involved, it would look exactly like senile dementia, or a psychotic break."

The pencil snapped in Lilah's lovely hands. "Oh. Yes, I can see how that would be very useful. But you say we only have notes."

"The complete spell itself is supposed to be recorded in the Compendium. It was Danetti's contribution before he vanished." Circe laughed. "The ancients had a habit of disappearing without warning. They didn't take nearly the care and precautions with their sorcery that we do nowadays."

"Well, modern magic." Lilah laughed with him.

"So you can see why I've been so upset by this. It could be an important contribution."

"Yes, I can see that. I'll do everything I can to

help out. And as you know, Circe"—it didn't hurt to remind him where the real power was here—"that's quite a bit. We should have that book for you in the next few days. Can you wait that long?"

He'd have to, whether he knew it or not.

"I suppose so. I can occupy my time balancing your budget, can't I?"

They shared another laugh.

After a few more pleasantries, the conversation ended. Lilah examined her list, and crossed off a couple of names. She could get some more use out of them; they were going to get that book for her.

She might not even flay them afterward. If the spell was really there . . . and worked.

Down in the depths of the Special Collections, Rutherford Circe set an old-fashioned telephone receiver gently into its cradle and rested one long, elegant hand on the cover of the Gilman auction collection catalog. Dear Lilah. So predictable.

She would never know the shock he had felt on seeing the listing when he had randomly paged through the book this morning. Of course he had never commissioned the associates to obtain it; how could he? How could anyone imagine such a treasure might be here?

He was certain the senior partners could imagine it, and hold the Librarian responsible for not obtaining it, if word got out. This way, though, he could enlist the aid of Special Projects to get his hands on it without bothering to use his own funds. Conveniently, he knew exactly which buttons to push: a mental restoration spell indeed! She'd never be able to resist that.

And the best part of all, of course: She was going to solve one other bothersome problem for him too. Because *his* sacrifice budget *had* been rather overrun lately.

CHAPTER NINE

Wesley had no idea where he was.

The last thing he remembered was leaning back on the worn leather couch with a drink in one hand and a good book in the other, opening it up and beginning to read. He hadn't heard any of the characteristic sounds of a dimensional portal opening, or smelled any supernatural effluvia. One minute he was absorbed in working his way through a patch of Old English, and the next he was . . .

Here.

And this was definitely not his apartment. For one thing, he no longer had that glass of whiskey handy. His CD player was gone; the rather whimsical Babylonian ziggurat on the coffee table—

"Get hold of yourself, man," he murmured. "It's just another dimension. It's not as if you haven't done this before."

And he had, of course, but that didn't make it any less unnerving to realize that this time he had no weapons, no spells, no idea how he had arrived, no idea how to get back, and even less than no idea why he seemed to be surrounded by bales and bales of paper.

At least he still had his glasses. And his shoes. Looking down, he saw he was standing on stiff, crackly ground, not concrete or even recognizable flooring. It was cream-colored with a spiderweb design all through it, like an American turquoise that Cordelia had shown him once—hundreds of fine black lines. Kingman's mine, if he recalled correctly, and he was sure he did. He was always good at trivia.

As he pivoted slowly, he saw that the surface extended in all directions as far as he could see, interrupted by stacks and walls of what looked like newsprint. The color varied from every shade of cream to glossy white. Every surface was marked in some fashion. There didn't seem to be any pattern or meaning to the marks, as far as he could tell.

For certain, none of the surfaces were marked with neon flashing signs marked EXIT.

Naturally.

He tried to think where he had heard of a dimension like this one, but came up blank. So, like a good occult researcher, he began to catalog the characteristics of the place.

He cast no shadow here. That more than anything unnerved him. He could see; there must be light from somewhere; he was still solid—a good pinch reassured him. When he looked straight up, he saw a flat, gray expanse that might be cloud cover or a gray ceiling fifty feet overhead. But there wasn't a sun in the sky, or a moon. Indeed, as far as he could tell, there simply wasn't a sky at all.

Nor was there anything else—living, undead things, or supernatural. He couldn't hear anything. The air was very dry; he could almost feel it parching his sinuses as he breathed. It carried no scent, except—

Yes, there *was* a smell in the air. A familiar and comforting smell. He breathed it deep into his lungs and let it go reluctantly.

The place smelled like a library. Or an old-fashioned bookstore, the kind that didn't come with biscotti and a coffee bar. A very old bookstore. Only without the dust. The kind of place he found the glorious summer he'd spent in Hay on Wye, a village in the West Country that had more bookstores than anyplace else in the U.K. He'd spent the whole summer in and out of places that smelled just like this, loaded himself up with books, and shipped them back to the Academy. He spent long evenings stretched out on the grass with a wisp of hay in his mouth, his chin propped up on his fists, a book in front of him and the world doing whatever it wished. It was the best summer of his entire life.

The smell of this place made him distrust it even more. If the place relaxed him, it meant he'd be off-guard. He was tempted to give a rousing "View halloo!" just to see what would happen, but long experience had taught him that if something did, it probably wouldn't be healthy. He quelled the impulse and instead looked around, trying to identify something he might use as a weapon if he was attacked, or someplace he might run and hide.

The place didn't seem quite as silent now. He could hear his own breathing, and the throb of blood in his eardrums, but when he held very still and controlled his breath as he had been taught so many years ago, he could now hear—*something*. Not close, he decided, but there was definitely something there. Something that wasn't interested in showing itself to him.

It made finding a weapon and shelter even more imperative.

Wesley's footsteps whispered and crunched on the surface—he had trouble thinking of it as ground, but he might as well, he told himself; it certainly wasn't a carpet. It was much more uneven than it looked, and there were lengthy dry sections where every step raised puffs of dust and the black spider-marks were barely noticeable. In the dustier places he found himself sneezing repeatedly, and he quickly started watching for the telltale puffs around his footfalls. He promptly backtracked, seeking a different approach or some way to avoid the region altogether.

It was by avoiding one such section that he discovered the wet ink.

He'd just backed out of one place that was not only dried out but looked as if it had collapsed from sheer age—a veritable canyon, twice as deep as he was tall and half again as wide, suspiciously smooth at the bottom, with much darker stains than he had seen elsewhere. He'd lost track of his arbitrary "north," and the horizon was obscured by rectangular stacks and bales of what might as well be filo dough. Off to one side he spotted a new configuration that looked like a pyramid of spools. Operating on the theory that anything unusual could provide a clue, he set off to explore that, hoping that at least he could spot his original destination from there.

On his way, as he passed yet another, very pale cream column, the closest of a near forest of such stacks, he noticed the familiar odor, overlaid on the bookstore smell. It struck him so forcibly that it stopped him in his tracks, and yet for a moment he couldn't identify it; he turned slowly, sniffing.

It was the strongest in the direction of the pale columns. He took a step toward them as if the scent were a pheromone-laden lure, and as he did so he recognized it for what it was, and he laughed at himself, but he followed it anyway.

That was how he discovered that the markings on the whitest columns were not mere spider-marks, but writing; and that the columns were actual stacks of pages. He entered the "forest" and realized that the stacks here were relatively untidy compared with the others he had passed, and the markings were more coherent. A corner of an actual page stuck out of one, and the markings that his eyes had come to pass over, unseeing, suddenly became meaningful. He reached for the page—a piece of green graph paper, he could now see—to try to pull it out to read what was on it, and the marks smeared on his fingers. It was still clear enough for him to read:

I am Tobey Cawber. I am a student of the Mysteries and these are

His fingers had smeared the rest.

Tobey Cawber? He was the owner of Beyond the Veil, one of Wes's haunts, a store that had closed down when he'd disappeared. Cawber was the man O'Flaherty wanted to talk to about books. Where had this come from? What was it doing here?

"Hey, you! Wha' d'ya think you're doing!"

He spun around to find an undersized, pimply kid, dressed in jeans and a grubby T-shirt, wearing a reversed California Angels baseball cap, staring belligerently at him. "Good lord. I didn't hear you—who are you?"

"My name's Artie. Who're you, and what do you think you're doing, taking my stuff? That's mine." The look on Artie's face was one of mulish desperation.

"I'm sorry." Wes held on to the sheet of paper and spread his arms wide to show he was no threat. Artie was even younger than his first perception, surely no more than fifteen. Perhaps he was one of the teen wizards Angel had been looking for. Maybe he was one of the ones who'd gotten away from the dimensional monster in the Horse Park. "My name's Wesley. I'm afraid I don't know where we are, or how I got here. Can you tell me? What is this place?"

Artie stared at him suspiciously. "I don't have to tell you nothin'."

"No, of course not." Wesley lowered his hands slowly, gesturing at the other stacks of paper. "Are all of these yours?"

Artie hesitated, and then said, too quickly, "Yeah. They're all mine. So you better leave them alone. And you better get out of here, before—"

He stopped, trembling.

"Before what?" Wesley asked gently.

Artie shook his head so hard, the baseball cap almost came off his head.

"Artie, this says 'Tobey Cawber.'"

"That's my uncle Tobey! You give that back!" Artie's voice rose to an almost hysterical scream, but he remained standing where he was, still trembling. Wes couldn't tell whether he was shaking with fear or with the effort to keep from lunging at him and the smeared green paper in his hand. "You give that back," he repeated, this time in a whisper. "Please. That's my uncle Tobey."

Wesley glanced at the smeared paper, at the boy whose eyes shone with the effort not to spill tears.

Slowly, he extended his hand, and held the paper out to the boy.

Artie snatched it from his hand and smoothed it against his chest. His head was ducked down so Wes could no longer see his face. He didn't need to in order to know that the boy was crying. "It's Uncle Tobey," Artie said again, his fingers stroking the wrinkled page. "It's all messed up. Uncle To—"

"Artie!" Another voice, a man's, from not far away but out of sight, urgent, warning. "It's coming! Hide!"

Artie's head snapped up, and he looked around frantically, wiping moisture out of his eyes. "You brought it here! You're new, it smells you! Get out of here, get *out*!" He spun around and ran back into the forest of paper columns.

Now Wes could hear something coming as well—something huge, from the sound of it—crashing through the paper trees. The sound seemed to echo against the sky, so that he couldn't tell exactly where it was coming from. He tried to see, but these trees had no branches to wave to show him direction. The columns and stacks of paper were thick around him at this point, and he couldn't see past them.

He nearly broke the arm that reached out to yank him back behind a column, before realizing that it was a human arm and not a demon's.

"Quiet!" a voice said in his ear. "For sanity's sake, man, stay quiet!"

He could hear running footsteps, several sets, as if a whole cadre of observers had taken to their heels. But the sounds of one pair of pounding feet seemed to be fainter, then louder again, and then the sound was almost on top of them, and Wesley pulled free of the restraining arm to look around the flimsy barrier and see what was happening.

Artie was back in the little clearing, clinging to the piece of green graph paper, and he was holding it out with both hands, as if offering it, to a monster that shimmered and towered over him, rearing up on a series of many knobby, claw-footed legs while reaching out with two more toward the boy. Wesley blinked. He was certain he had never seen this demon illustrated in one of the dozens of reference books either at home or in the Angel Investigations office, but it was somehow familiar nonetheless.

It was dark gray, with silver highlights, shaped something like a teardrop or perhaps a segmented gray carrot, with twisting antenna on both ends of its body, but particularly the rounded end facing the boy. There, they surrounded a shifting, devouring maw. He estimated its total length at more than fifty feet, not counting the antennae lashing through the air.

The long, pointed end of the demon stretched horizontally across the ground, the front third rising up with multiple legs clawing at the air while the rest of its legs—he couldn't tell how many—pulled the thing forward. As it moved it roared, its jaws opening wide. He could almost feel the heat of the monster's breath; the smell, an uncanny mixture of old blood and older ink, demon bile and decay, radiated from the thing.

The creature was hard to look at, as if it was shifting between dimensions even as it moved. But the damage it wreaked in this dimension was all too effective; shrieking, delighted, it passed through a column of paper twelve feet tall, four feet on a side, and the column was gone. It twisted on its scaled body, the legs digging in as if for purchase, and raised itself even higher. It was hanging in the air over the boy's head.

Artie held out the paper to the monster, as if in appeasement. Wes could see his hands shaking.

The thing reached out, obscenely flexible, folding

itself over the boy as if bowing to him, and took the green page—not with the free legs, but with its mouth, delicately sucking it up, drawing the letters out from the page in a swirl of black mist as if it were a perfume to inhale. Artie's arms dropped, relieved that his offering was accepted, and Wes heard the voice behind him mutter, "Oh, the poor fool. He thinks that will stop it."

The monster reared up again and fell on the boy like an avalanche, its mouth expanding to ten times its original size and enveloping him. As the mouth closed over Artie, Wesley clearly heard the *crunch* and *splat* of broken bones and popping organs. Globs of blood and tissue squeezed between the circle of fangs and splattered over the surrounding columns.

The crunching went on for a very long time.

The boy didn't even have time to scream.

Wesley's stomach heaved. His hands opened and closed, agonized in their emptiness.

"Quiet!" the voice behind him warned, very softly. "It can hear us. It can smell us. Even through all the blood."

The thing stretched out on the ground, rolling in what looked very much like ecstasy, and it was firmly in this dimension, weighted down by its meal, making a stained impression in the ground.

Where there had once been a boy was nothing but gore soaked into the surrounding paper; a single sneaker; and the California Angels cap, flung aside as its owner was devoured.

As the demon rolled across the paper landscape, the stains disappeared, as if absorbed through its surface. Wesley stood frozen, watching, as the demon rolled closer, crushing the surrounding trees.

The grip on his arm bit deep into his biceps, warning him to keep still. As if he *could*.

Then the monster paused. Slowly, it began to untwist from its contorted position, and straighten. Its enormous, gray, segmented flank was less than six feet from him. He could have taken a long step forward and touched it. Stabbed it, if he had had the means.

The hand on Wesley's arm began to tug him back, deeper into the paper trees.

He shrugged it away, terrified, transfixed, needing to know what would happen next.

The demon rose up again, as it had just before it fell on Artie. Its round eye swept past him, solid black and glistening, but somehow it didn't see him. It swayed away, like a cobra preparing to strike, but there was nothing left that he could see to strike at. The surface before it was smooth and clean where it had rolled. Only a few red splashes remained on the tree next to Wesley to show where a human being had died.

The demon moved backward, still swaying, as if

examining the ground before it for imperfections, or leftovers.

There were none.

The demon roared again, a different note this time—a long, high scream that ended in a cough. The antennae over its head arched downward as it bent itself forward, low enough for the antenna to actually touch the ground, and the demon lifted itself on its multiple short legs so that no part of the massive body still remained in contact with the ground.

It coughed.

It coughed again, and then vomited suddenly, a stream of stinking, glistening blackness from the round jaws onto the pristine white surface. Then it folded itself over once more, and the antennae touched the pool of black. They began moving, jerkily, back and forth, from the pool of black vomit to the white surface, over and over again. As they did so, the pool began to shrink.

The demon shifted itself backward, and Wesley realized suddenly that if he remained where he was, he would once again be even with the demon's eye. It would be too much to hope that it would fail to see him a second time. He let the unseen owner of the hand on his arm guide him away, deeper into the remaining paper trees. He refused to go any farther than the second row. He had to see what was going on.

The demon stopped moving. As far as Wesley could see, the pool of black fluid was gone.

It shook itself, twisted in place, and began crawling off. Just before it would have left his line of sight, the demon shimmered. Then it was gone.

"Dear lord," Wes whispered. He was not a man much given to prayer, but the expression seemed called for under the circumstances. "What *is* that thing?"

"That is a Bookwyrm," the voice behind him said with pedantic relish. "Or, more precisely, *the* Bookwyrm. The demon that inhabits the Red Compendium."

Wes turned to his rescuer. "Who are y—dear lord."

The man before him was at least thirty-five years his senior, five inches shorter, with sharp hazel eyes and a rather large nose. Wesley hadn't laid eyes on him for years, but there was no mistaking him.

He had been one of Wesley's idols for as long as he could remember, even though his son had been one of his worst enemies.

"Mr. O'Flaherty? I thought you were dead."

"Wyndam-Pryce, isn't it?" Adrian had inherited the lean physique, the green eyes, the high cheekbones. This man's hair had more red in it, however, and much more gray. And where his son's eyes glinted with malice and mischief, his own sparkled with wry, sad humor.

"Dead?" Gabriel O'Flaherty continued. "Really? And why would you think that? If past evidence was any indication, I should simply have disappeared without a trace, just as so many others did." The older man smiled grimly.

"The explosion. I thought you were killed in the explosion."

"And what explosion would that be?" Gabriel had passed along to his son the habit of sticking his hands in his pockets, tilting his head to one side like a fascinated bird.

"The explosion—don't you know?" Wesley was still in shock from seeing the demon eat Artie. On top of that, he had just met a dead man, who apparently didn't know about the circumstances of his own death.

"Evidently not, Mr. Wyndam-Pryce. Please elucidate."

He really didn't know how to proceed.

"A—a couple of—just recently. There was an explosion. At Council headquarters."

"Was anyone hurt?" The humor was gone out of the elder O'Flaherty's eyes.

"Not—not Adrian," Wesley said hastily. "Your son—he's fine, I know, I saw him just a few hours ago." Was it a few hours? he wondered suddenly. He had no idea how time moved here relative to his own dimension. "But the others—nearly all of them were killed when the building collapsed."

Gabriel's eyes closed, and he swayed.

"Sir, I'm terribly sorry."

"All? Quentin? Alaine?"

Wesley had to stop and think to realize that the man was referring to the Head of the Council and his second, who had been one of his teachers at the Academy. "I'm afraid that Mr. Travers and Madame Shearer were among the casualties, yes."

"Rupert?"

Wes blinked. Who was Rupert—oh, of course. Giles. He'd never thought of the Sunnydale Watcher, the last Active Watcher, by his first name. "No, Mr. Giles survived."

It was going to be a long, complicated explanation, Wesley could tell. And he didn't feel up to it at the moment.

"Sir, if you don't mind. Where are we, exactly?"

"Don't you know where you are yet?"

"Not exactly, no."

"Come with me." Still pale, Gabriel O'Flaherty led him out of the shelter of the stacks and columns of paper, out to where the demon had vomited and scrabbled on the ground. "Look."

Above the stained-glass windows are other, broad windows of clear glass. Through the clear glass comes pure, untrammeled sunlight. It washes out the colors that would otherwise paint the dark wood of the floor.

"You will go through that door," Madame Shearer is saying, "and go up the spiral staircase that will lead you to the catwalk. You will go out on the catwalk and space yourselves as evenly as possible around it."

"Madame," O'Flaherty says, "you said we were going to assist a Watcher? What are we supposed to do?"

"Who's the Watcher?" Leslye-Flindshym wants to know.

You do not hear the response, if any; you are already following directions, and are winding your way up the steps that circle all the way around the room.

You have taken up a position, looking down three stories, and you see your professor standing in the center of the room, looking up. She is spacing your classmates out with small gestures and nods, ensuring that you are all equidistant. You still do not know what you are supposed to do, what you are here to do.

Suddenly you are afraid, afraid to your very soul. What if . . . what if Father was right all along?

And you can't do what needs to be done.

Gabriel pointed down at the ground where the demon's antennae had frantically scratched away. His index finger was extended like the Ghost of Christmas Past; and, like Ebenezer Scrooge, Wesley did not want to see what was revealed.

There were words where the antennae had scrambled the vomit into the paper ground, and he could not help but read them. These words were in English, and he could not *not* read:

I am Artie Cawber. I am fourteen years old. I go to school at Burbank High. . . .

CHAPTER TEN

"You're inside the book." Gabriel tugged his sleeve, pulling him along, away from the demonic inscription. "I tried to keep poor Artie away from the Wyrm ever since he got here, but it was inevitable, I fear. We've been trying to keep him away from the Wyrm, but he's desperate to find his uncle. *Was* desperate, I should say.

"He's not going to keep the beast fed for long, though. We've got to get out of its way before it gets on your track again."

"With all due respect, sir, what the devil are you talking about?" He thought he knew. He didn't want to know. Wesley had never had much patience with denial; it was a curious sensation to find himself wallowing deep in it.

Gabriel shook his head and led him at a quick trot deeper into the paper forest, past the pyramid of scrolls and through a small garden of pamphlets to another, denser thicket. Wes estimated they had been gone at least a couple of miles before they finally came to a stop in a small clearing. This place was different from the rest; instead of paper, rocks were piled up, arranged into a makeshift table, chairs, and what might have been benches or even beds. Wes stepped over to examine them: Yes, they were engraved with worn lines of cuneiform, hieratic, and hieroglyphic writing—more ancient scripts he could not begin to read.

"I repeat, sir: What the devil are you talking about?" he said, seating himself on a pile of tablets and tracing the indentations in the stone. He was desperately cold inside, and felt like he would never, ever be warm again.

"This is the book itself, the *Compendium of auntient Graymarye,*" the older man said. Wesley looked up to see Gabriel seating himself at the table in the center of the clearing. Gabriel saw the expression on his face and sighed. "You are only the latest to have opened the book, Wyndam-Pryce, and been pulled into it by the demon you have just seen—the Bookwyrm. It feeds on us. Feeds on the magic we know."

His voice was taking on the rhythm of the lecture hall now, and Wes had the sensation that years had fallen away from both of them, that they were back at the Academy and he was hearing a lecture, something he would be tested on tomorrow, or next week. It wasn't real. It was only a dry history lecture in a paneled classroom with a Grinling Gibbons fireplace mantel and centuries-old portraits of famous Watchers hanging proudly upon the walls.

"The Red Compendium has always had the reputation of being the greatest collection of spells known to human sorcery, but no one seems to have possessed it for very long. You have just seen the reason why. The book attracts magicians, sorcerers; if you open it, read it, if you have knowledge the Wyrm doesn't possess . . . you end up here. And the Compendium moves on to attract the Wyrm's next victim."

"Are you saying Artie—that child—was a sorcerer?" Wesley couldn't quite keep the disbelief from his voice. It was easier to focus on Artie than on the idea of being inside a book. "He couldn't have been. And if he knew what the thing would do, why did he go back?"

Gabriel shook his head. "No, Artie was no sorcerer. He didn't see the Wyrm take his uncle; we told him what had happened—suitably edited for his age, of course. That might have been our mistake. He seemed to think the Wyrm could give him his uncle back.

"As for how he got here—somewhere along the line he picked up the book and got sucked in by sheer accident, I believe. There have been several such accidents over time. Which simply proves the Wyrm is not omniscient. That's the only reason we've managed to stay alive this long."

"'We'? How many are there of you? And how can we get out of here?"

"I won't tell you how many I know of," Gabriel said. "If the Wyrm catches you, you won't be able to pass along the information. As for getting out— my dear boy, no one has ever escaped from the Red Compendium. Look about you. Look at the very ground beneath your feet. Every mark you see is a spell affixed in this book by someone who has been devoured by that demon you just saw.

"Over the centuries it has captured dozens, perhaps hundreds, of wizards, magicians, mages, and students of the occult who have made the mistake of seeking the knowledge it uses as its lure. It feeds on our need to know, and on *what* we know, and uses that knowledge to bring in still more victims. Once here, it hunts us down. Eventually it sucks us dry and turns us into spells on the page, our only remaining life the magic we exert when someone casts the spells. All of our knowledge becomes a part of the Bookwyrm and is compiled into the book. It becomes more powerful with every human it devours.

"Look around you. You'll see Rahman Ali here. Donovan Reese. Li Sing Oh. !kee Ta. Michelle Ten Dove. The Fourth Singer of Songs. All of them were exactly like me—exactly like you. We've all heard about the famous Red Compendium, and not one of us could resist the temptation of reading it if we were offered the chance. Every one of us made the mistake of opening this book. All of us fell to the Wyrm.

"I suspected as much, you know. Even told the Council. But when the book showed up in the Library, I couldn't resist taking a quick look at it any more than any of the others could. And I've been here ever since."

"Did you know about the Wyrm?" Wesley asked. "When you read the book?"

"Oh, of course not. I should have—the book had to get its power from somewhere, didn't it? But all I had to go on was the common theme: Someone major in our world vanishes without a trace, and rumors begin that that person's most important spells are in the Compendium."

"And so off we all go in hot pursuit of the perfect text," Wesley said to himself.

"Exactly."

Wes looked around at the tablets, the ground, the columns. "That's what all this is, then? The accumulated knowledge, the essence of all those men and women? And demons, too?"

Gabriel shook his head. "Never seen a demon here. I don't think the Wyrm's glamour works on them the way it does on us. Maybe that's where the book goes when it's missing. Maybe it's in demon hands."

Wes nodded. "And I imagine there would be those who would be perfectly happy to stay, if it weren't for the Wyrm."

Gabriel laughed. "Of course we would. It's a plain paradise, boy. Imagine being able to read for as long as you liked, never having to stop to eat or drink or any of those untidy distractions. You'd never run out of subjects, either. It's not all arcana, you know. There's some delightful poetry. Philosophy. Scientific speculation. Sorcerers don't just sit around all day doing magic." He looked as if he would be one of those happy to stay. "Some of us spend a lot of time just looking for ways to get rid of the Wyrm. Of course, if it weren't for the Wyrm, the place probably couldn't exist. And getting out, well—"

"No one's ever gotten out of the book?"

"Don't you think if there was a way out of here, we would have found it by now? The Wyrm's victims have been trying to escape for centuries. If anyone had succeeded, the book would have been burned long ago."

"And thus the Wyrm has been eating for centuries," Wesley said.

Gabriel nodded. "Gaining power with every bite, we reckon. Of course, it gets the names of likely victims when it ingests us, and then it sends itself on and on and on. It gets better at it all the time. We think that eventually it wants everyone, every creative soul, to write into itself. And if it keeps it up, it will."

Wesley went cold with horror, remembering the eagerness with which he had claimed the book, the satisfaction he'd felt when he'd sat down to open it. The gentle tingle in his fingers when he'd first found it in that box of books in the auction. And then something else occurred to him as well. "Sir—*you* were the keeper of the entire Watchers Library. You must have read nearly every volume in the collection."

Gabriel O'Flaherty stared at him without blinking, an expression so reminiscent of his son that it sent chills down Wesley's spine. "Yes, of course. I imagine that once the Wyrm manages to eat *me*, it will be pretty near unstoppable. It does rather add an incentive to staying alive."

"Yes, I imagine it would," Wesley murmured.

There are thirteen members of the sixth form, you realize abruptly. You have known this, of course, ever since Rensey dropped out at the beginning of the term, but it has never bothered you before. You have never considered yourself superstitious, but you are aware of the significance of the number.

On one side of you is Adrian O'Flaherty. On the other, Michael Davidowitz. O'Flaherty is intent, for a change; he's not making silly comments or fooling around. Davidowitz is peering nearsightedly at everything except the other people in the room. You wonder what he expects to see.

"You have spent six years studying," Madame Shearer says, her voice carrying clearly to the catwalk. "You have read history and ritual in each of those six years. Today you will see what that history and ritual mean." She raises her hand; she has some kind of remote control. She is pointing at the windows. She pivots, and as she does so a set of dark shades unrolls over each clear window.

The room darkens. The only light now is filtered through the stained glass. The patterns on the floor stand out starkly. They crawl over Madame Shearer like monsters.

Another door in the Circle Room opens. The dozen-plus-one students lean over the railing, straining to see in the warped light below.

"Ladies and gentlemen," Madame Shearer says, her voice clipped now as if in distaste, "I present Miss Gillie Karrens. Miss Karrens was a Watcher on field duty who was responsible for the welfare and training of a Slayer-in-Waiting. She is here today to demonstrate to you some of the more practical aspects of your six years of study. Please feel free to render any assistance you feel advisable."

With that, Madame Shearer steps through a door, and it shuts behind her. Another door opens, *and a woman enters the room. She is tall, and thin, with red hair, and looks about uncertainly. You realize she cannot see you against the light.*

"Was responsible?" you think. And why did Madame Shearer introduce the woman before she actually entered the room?

What assistance?

And what enemy?

And yet another door opens—this will be the fifth door in the room, you realize—and someone else comes in the room.

You hear Leslye-Flindshym draw breath to call out something to Karrens.

And then the "someone else" becomes Vampire.

CHAPTER ELEVEN

Lilah Morgan looked at the pile of books in front of her with something between distaste and dismay. The two members of the Wolfram & Hart security staff standing in front of her were at attention, trying not to look at the mess on the glossy surface of her mahogany desk.

"Well," she said, consulting the catalog, "this is the right lot. You're certain you got everything?"

They couldn't be certain unless they'd brought in the whole damned apartment, she thought.

"I think we did," the more senior of the security pair said. "The box was beside a chair in the living room, and we brought in the box and all the books around the chair. It appeared that he had just started going through the contents when he left."

"I see." It was a fair inference. Of course, he could very well have taken the book with him. "No one has seen him anywhere?"

"No, ma'am," the other security man said. He had demon blood; it showed in the red sclera of his eyes. "We put a trace on him as soon as we found out he wasn't in the location. Nothing has come back yet."

She nodded. As an afterthought, she asked, "Did anyone see you searching the place?"

The senior man looked insulted. "Of course not, Ms. Morgan. We did our job the way we're supposed to. I promise you, nobody saw us in there. We didn't leave any fingerprints, either."

"I'm sure you didn't." Security staff at Wolfram & Hart were efficient. If they weren't, they didn't last long. "All right. If I think of anything else, I'll call you. You can go now."

The two of them left, not without an audible breath of relief.

Lilah poked at a stack of musty tomes. "I should have known it would be you, Wesley," she said softly.

Of course it would be Wes who'd bought the box. She'd known he and his Watcher pal O'Flaherty had been at the auction; who else would manage to thwart Wolfram & Hart so neatly? It had been downright pleasant to order security to go after him.

If he had been in the apartment, they were instructed to do decorative damage, but nothing permanent. She'd spent a very agreeable couple of hours imagining an angry Wesley tied and bound while a full security team went through his place with a fine-tooth comb.

Well, they'd gone through it, all right. And this is what she got for it. A bunch of books that might or might not include what she was looking for.

She couldn't very well ask Circe to come up and identify his bloody Red Compendium for her. He'd just take it away, and her opportunity would be gone.

The trouble was, none of these books were red, exactly. The new ones she could sort to one side, reasonably sure this fabulous grimoire wasn't disguised as a paperback guide to pop astrology. But the old ones were all dark, grimy with decades and centuries of use. They might all have been red, once. She didn't feel like getting her hands dirty looking through the whole stack.

If nothing else, Wolfram & Hart understood the value of specialists. And Lilah had her own list of outside consultants when she didn't want to use in-house staff. She picked up the phone and made a call.

Angel cut the connection and suppressed the urge to snarl with annoyance.

"Still not answering?" Fred asked.

"Still not answering," he confirmed. "I don't like it. I thought he'd be back here after the auction. We still have a problem we haven't solved. At least, I think we haven't solved it. Cordy?"

Cordelia shrugged. "I got nothing." She had a red, blue, and gold scarf wrapped around her hair, and she was trying to polish a banister. It wasn't going well.

"So maybe we broke up our little Hogwarts wanna-bes," Gunn said. "What's left of them, that is. After that last try, maybe they finally figured out that the magic ain't fun."

Angel thought about it. "Yeah, maybe. But why hasn't Wes checked in?"

"Maybe he and his Watcher buddy are cruisin'."

Fred snorted. "I don't think Wes and his 'Watcher buddy' are all that buddy."

Cordelia tossed down the polishing rag in disgust. "I agree. Those two were definitely not *Road to Morocco*. Or anyplace else. I think the only reason Wes brought him over here was to see the look on his face when he introduced you, Angel."

"That's the truth," Gunn said. "That was a setup, pure and simple, and our man English was having himself a real good time springing it on this guy."

Angel concurred. As much as he didn't like being the bait in someone else's trap—or the trap in someone else's trap—it was obvious that Wesley hadn't warned O'Flaherty about what he was walking into. "So Wes isn't too tight with the guy. Anybody got any ideas why this O'Flaherty looked Wes up? He was sharp enough about playing keep-away from Lorne."

The staff of Angel Investigations stared blankly at one another.

"Some Watcher stuff, maybe?" Cordy offered. "Would Giles know?"

"Maybe." Angel hit redial on the phone and listened to the ring—ring—ring and then the clipped voice, no nonsense, no wasted syllables: *Wesley Wyndam-Pryce. Leave a message.* "We'll leave asking Giles until later."

He didn't want to ask Giles. He wasn't sure that Giles had ever really forgiven him for killing his lover when he had lost his regained soul and become Angelus, back in Sunnydale.

And besides, when he had to talk to Giles, he wanted to talk to Buffy, and he couldn't do that.

"That's it," he said. "I'm going by his place."

"I'll go with you," Gunn said at once.

"No, you need to stay here in case something comes up." Angel nodded at Cordelia. Gunn wasn't back to form yet; his arm still bothered him, even though he didn't want to admit it. The bandages had been off for less than a day.

"Yeah," Cordy said. "Vision Girl backup, please." She tossed the polishing cloth down and glared at the banister. "Glossy wood backup too, if that doesn't work out. This just sucks."

"You're using wax, not oil," Fred told her. "It's easier with oil."

"And oil makes it easier to burn the place to the

ground for insurance too," Gunn supplied help-
fully. "Not that I'd know anything about that," he
added hastily, off Angel's look.

"I won't be gone long. Just swing by and see
what's the what there," Angel said. It was definitely
time for him to get away from his team again. They
were his friends—his family—but like all families,
sometimes enough was too much, especially when
they started squabbling about inconsequentials.

It was after sunset, which gave him an opportunity to drive the convertible. He would have taken
the long way, through the bright lights and sleaze
of the Strip, just to watch the tourists and hookers
and wanna-be movie stars, but it had been three
days since they had heard from Wesley, and he was
even more worried than he wanted to admit.

He slowed down as he passed the park where
Justine had cut Wes's throat. That seemed so long
ago, now! The apartment was close by; he pulled
up in front of it and sat for a moment, looking
around.

The street was quiet, tree branches nearly meeting over it. Two hundred feet away, a man stood
waiting while a dog investigated a burned-out
streetlamp. Lights glowed through drawn curtains
of the bank of apartments on either side of the
road.

Nothing out of the ordinary. Nothing suspicious.
No reason for him to feel uneasy.

He felt uneasy anyway.

He got out of the car, and the sound of the door closing made the dog look up. The wind was in the wrong direction, and it couldn't smell him. Before it could get any closer, he went up the walk to Wes's door and rang the bell.

No answer.

He knocked.

No answer.

He tried the door. It was locked; that presented no problem in and of itself. Before he twisted it off its hinges, however, he hesitated, and pulled out the cell phone.

"Angel Investigations."

"Cordy? Does anybody there have a key to Wes's place?"

"He's not there, huh?" There was a muffled conversation on the other end; then Cordelia got back on the line. "Nope, no key. But Resource Guy will be right over. Hang in there, boss."

He had to "hang in there" in the shadows, waiting, as the dog walker went by. As the dog came downwind of him and passed the convertible, it lifted its head and peered into the shadows, yelped and cringed, yanking its owner back in the opposite direction. Angel watched as the dog's owner stumbled, then chased the frantic animal down the street and out of sight. "Smart pooch," he murmured.

Once upon a time, Angel could have entered Wes's apartment with no difficulty. But after the incident where Angel had tried to strangle Wes as he lay helpless in his hospital bed, Wes had cast the spells that retracted the invitation. Angel couldn't cross his threshold.

Gunn showed up twenty minutes later. "Locked, huh?"

"Yep."

"That could be a good thing. Or not. Let's see now." Gunn examined the locks on the front door, then moved to the windows.

"And here I thought you were one of the good guys," Angel said as Gunn fiddled with a window lock.

"I am a good guy with many diverse skills," Gunn replied with dignity as the window slid open. "Check this out, please. Has our man put any nasty magickal surprises on this window?"

Angel examined the opening. Sure enough, there were some protections in place. "Nothing that's going to affect you, I think," he said. "These are designed to repel occult attacks."

"You *think*?" Gunn didn't look particularly reassured, but he took a deep breath and lifted out the screen. No alarms, physical or otherwise, went off. "Here we go, then. Tell Mamma I loved her." He swung a leg over the sill.

Again, no alarms. Relieved, Angel moved back to the front door.

Moments later it swung open, to reveal an angry and anxious Gunn. "Man, we got us a problem here. Look."

Angel peered through the door into Wes's living room. It looked as if a tornado had hit the place. The couch and chair had been turned upside down, and the cushions had been ripped apart. The bookshelves were empty, their contents scattered on the floor. The coffee table was shoved against the far wall. The sound system looked as if someone had taken an ax to it, and broken CDs and jewel boxes were scattered everywhere. Even the pictures had been ripped from the walls.

"What the *hell* happened here?" Angel said.

"I don't know," Gunn said. "But the bedroom's even worse. Feather pillows make a real mess. The only good thing is, I don't see blood anywhere, so—"

"Oh, he's definitely still alive, wherever he is," Angel said, his hands splayed against the door frame like a mime trying to fight his way out of a box. "That much we know for sure. If he was dead, I could come in." He couldn't smell any blood spilled in the apartment either. That was good. Wasn't it?

Gunn winced.

"Is there anything that shows how long ago this might have happened?" Angel demanded.

"I'll check around. You could look in his mailbox. Er, couldn't you?"

"*That* I can do."

He found advertising circulars, savings coupons, letters from banks offering amazing deals on credit cards. He took everything and went back to the apartment before someone else came in to pick up his or her mail. Fortunately, he didn't have to worry about leaving fingerprints; his weren't on file anywhere.

He met Gunn coming out the door. "Anything?"

The light from the streetlamp played across his shaved head as Gunn shook it in denial. "Nothing. They came in through the back—it was standing wide open; I could have saved myself a trip through the window. Whoever it was knew what they were doing. They went through everything. But there's nothing to show that he was here at the time, and Wes would have put up a decent fight even if he'd been surprised."

"That, he would have," Angel agreed.

"So the last we heard from him was when he called after taking O'Flaherty to Caritas. Sometime between then and now, this happened, and nobody's heard a word from him since."

"A fair summary."

"So where's Wesley? And is he wearing a funny wool hat, suspenders, and a striped shirt?"

Angel looked at Gunn as if he had completely lost his mind. "A *funny wool hat and a striped shirt*?"

"I guess your mamma didn't read you those books. Never mind."

Since Gunn knew perfectly well how long ago Angel's "mamma" had shuffled off this mortal coil—and how—Angel decided that this was a pop culture reference he simply wasn't going to follow up on. From the look on Gunn's face as soon as the words were out of his mouth, he preferred that Angel not follow up on it either.

"I didn't see any signs of who did it," he added hastily. "Not your average break-in opportunity. Besides, the sound system's pretty nice, and it's still there. It looks like somebody was looking for something pretty specific."

"*Dammit!*" The vampire slammed a fist into—and through—the brick of a retaining wall. Gunn winced. "I want to get *in* there and look around."

"Hey, don't you think I did—," Gunn started to protest.

Angel shook his head. "No, you know it's not that. I just want to see for myself. And I can't get in there. I can't walk in through an open door."

Gunn simply stared at him, not commenting on that. *Vampire.* He didn't say it out loud, but the word was loud in his eyes. And, of course, the minor issues Wesley and Angel were still in the process of working out—mostly resolved, but every once in a while, a reminder like this . . .

That was something else Angel chose not to respond to.

"Let's go see if his car is still in the garage," Gunn suggested. "That'll at least tell us if he was here when it happened. Maybe he's just taking a trip with his buddy, chasing more artifacts or something."

"Yeah, right. Check the car. Good."

The car, unfortunately, was still in the reserved parking space in off-street parking.

"Next steps?"

"I think," Angel said, "I want to have a little discussion with Mr. Adrian O'Flaherty."

"How long have you been here, sir?" Wesley asked, looking around the little camp. He could see at least half a dozen rumpled areas that held what looked like the imprints of sleeping bodies—he devoutly hoped they had been sleeping—and loose pages lying about in small stacks beside them, as if some of the columns had been torn apart for reading material. There was no sign of a campfire, though, or any food or water.

"I'm not certain," the older man said. "Time passes, you know. I hardly notice, as long as the Wyrm isn't about. What's the date? Or, more precisely, what was the date when you opened the book? And where were you? How did the book get you?"

Wesley checked his watch, only to find that it had stopped at some point. "I was at home. It was—" He had to stop and think about the date. Tuesday had been—oh, never mind.

Besides, he was struck by the phrasing—*How did the book get you?* not *Where did you get it?* "I found the book at an auction—Tobey Cawber's stock was dispersed there. So we are definitely in another dimension, then?"

The senior O'Flaherty considered. "That's our consensus. It would almost have to be, wouldn't it? One cannot tell time by the sun, here, because there is no sun. And there's no food, either, though one doesn't miss it. We sleep, a little. But that's unreliable. One of us tries to stay alert, watchful, but it's difficult sometimes with all this temptation about."

He smiled wryly, eyes shining behind his glasses, and one hand reached out to touch a yellowed column, riffle its surface gently, separating what Wesley could now see as irregular sheets of papyrus. "Dreadful, isn't it. But there is so *much* here. You have no idea. Works we've only had hints of, things lost since the Great Fires of Alexandria and Rome, here for the reading. One never knows what one will find.

"That's the greatest danger," he added abruptly, pulling his hand away and rubbing it against his side as if to obliterate the feel of the pages. "One becomes utterly absorbed in something, and then before one knows it, the Wyrm is upon you. It's quite too bad that we've lost Artie. He didn't really like to read, you see. Made an excellent watchman."

Wesley looked around again, trying to sense someone, anyone else, in the landscape of stacks. "How many people are caught in here?" He considered his choice of words in light of the endless landscape of pages. "How many are still alive, I mean?"

He shook his head. "Not as many as there were, boy. No one sits down for a nice, comfy read with a grenade in hand, you know. None of us so far, anyway. We haven't managed to find a way to kill it. There aren't many of us left, and fewer all the time. It finds us, and eats us, and spits us out onto the pages—everything we know gets written up. That's where it all comes from, you know. For millennia. From us."

Wesley remembered the feel of fresh ink on his fingertips, and suppressed a shudder.

"It knows you're here, boy. It's going to be after you. You're fresh blood. New experiences, new spells. We think it already has absorbed everything we know when we fall into the book, but in order to write, it has to—"

"Eat us."

O'Flaherty nodded sadly. "It won't get much out

of that poor Artie Cawber," he said. "Not much at all. It's going to be hungry."

"How many of you—us—are there in the book? Still alive, I mean?"

O'Flaherty sighed. "Now, with Artie gone? Eight or nine, perhaps. I'm not certain. It's a large place, you know, a very, very large place. The Wyrm has eaten a lot of people over the centuries. There could be a lot more about that I've never seen."

"But you don't think so, do you?"

O'Flaherty chuckled. "Shrewd one, aren't you? No, I don't. The Wyrm hangs about us too much these days. That tells me there aren't as many snacks available for it. People don't read anymore, you know—at least, not our sort of thing. So it hunts us."

Wesley ran his hands over the piles of paper stacked around him. "All of this is from—"

"Yes."

There was a moment of appalled silence.

Then, behind them, someone called out, and Wesley raised his hands to his ears as the air pressure changed, and Gabriel O'Flaherty gasped.

Wesley spun to see the Wyrm charging toward them, mouth agape.

"I'm sorry, I really have no idea what you're talking about." O'Flaherty was sitting in one of the leather chairs, but under the pose of studied indifference. Angel could see the tension in his leg muscles, the balance just slightly forward instead of relaxed and back against the deep cushion. "Pryce dropped me off at my hotel this past Tuesday night after we left that club, Caritas. I haven't seen or heard from him since."

O'Flaherty had come to the hotel at Cordy's invitation; she had asked for help in translating a text and had put years of flirting practice into it. As soon as he had stepped in the door, he had been escorted to a chair instead. Angel could hear his heart beating faster, but nothing in his expression betrayed what he was feeling as Angel Investigations surrounded him.

"And what have *you* been doing since?"

Serene hazel eyes met hard brown ones. "Visiting parks, museums, bookstores, the various tourist attractions in your fair city. The museum is quite striking."

"I hear you tried to meet most of the staff at the UCLA main library."

"My father was a librarian. I spoke to some of his acquaintances among them."

Angel decided to stop sparring. "Why are you here, O'Flaherty? What are you looking for?"

"Well, I didn't come here to be interrogated," he snapped back.

"Well, that's what's happening now, mister. So you'd better start talking!" Fred was ready to do some heavy hitting of her own.

A glitter of amusement crossed O'Flaherty's face. "What a ferocious hamster you are. I'm very sorry, sweetheart—"

Fred marched over to the weapons cabinet, got out a crossbow, and leveled it at him.

O'Flaherty raised an eyebrow. "Here, now!"

"And after that, she gets out the white-hot pincers," Cordy advised him. "I'd start talking, if I were you." She was standing with her arms crossed over her chest, looking grim. Looking as if the idea of white-hot pincers was really appealing.

"You're all utterly mad. I've told you I have nothing to do with this. I have no idea where he might be. And quite frankly, I don't care."

"So much for looking up old friends and fellow Watchers," Cordy snapped. "Why did you, anyway? You've dropped him like an ex-agent. Didn't he have what you're looking for?"

The look he gave her was considerably less friendly, Angel thought, because he'd fallen for her lure. Or perhaps it was the threat. "He didn't. Neither do you, darling. None of you have what I want, and I haven't got what you want. I suggest you let me go—"

"Hold the phone, guys and gals, and stop the presses!" The front door banged open—the Hyperion was too old to have hydraulic doors—and Lorne lunged in, breathless. He was dressed in show clothes, a dazzling dark red satin tuxedo that

Liberace would have itched to lace with crystals. On any other green-skinned demon, it would have reminded one irresistably of Christmas; on Krevlorneswath of the Deathwok Clan, late of Pylea, Host of Caritas, it was gorgeous, showy, and practically tasteful.

Lorne ran down the steps and grabbed at Angel's arm. "Good, everybody's here." He then noticed O'Flaherty sitting there, surrounded. "Well, not so good—he's here too. Oh, well. Angel-cakes, I've got news. Tonight, at the show—" He paused to catch his breath, and Fred, in full mommy mode, passed him a glass of water. "Bless you, sweet thing. Whew."

Every eye was on Lorne; O'Flaherty made a move to get up, very quietly. One dark hand on his shoulder rammed him back into the chair. Gunn had very wide peripheral vision.

"Lorne, we're kind of in the middle of something here. Wes is—"

"That's *it*, sweetie. That's what I've got to tell you. In a second. . . ." He took another gulp of the water and passed the glass back to Fred. "Thanks. I owe you a billion votes of gratitude. Now.

"Tonight, at the club. A couple of the kids from Wolfram and Hart showed up, and this time they were off the leash—"

"What do you mean, 'off the leash'?"

"Last time, Lilah of the Icy Heart was with

them. That woman could chill champagne at forty paces. But this time they were on their own. And I was doing the audience-tour thing, you know, where I go through the audience and let anybody sing who wants to. It doesn't take long, it's just sort of a quickie read—"

"We know, Lorne." Angel tried to keep the simmering impatience out of his voice. Lorne heard it anyway.

"Yes. Well. I was a table away, and I happened to overhear these two guys. One was trying to convince the other to sing for me. They were talking about a break-in. The one guy says, 'We'd better find out what Circe wants with it before Morgan gives it to him. It's our necks on the line.' And the other one says"—Lorne paused dramatically—"the other one says, 'But the green guy's gonna know it was Wyndam-Pryce's place, won't he?'"

"You're sure he said Wyndam-Pryce?"

"Of course I'm sure. It's not like it's a common name like Impof or Xyxlistif. But just in case, I had the bartender make their drinks a whole lot stronger than they thought they were. I was hoping to get more out of them. But nothing. Just a red book, and they were just as worried about this Circe guy as they were about our Miss Lilah."

"I thought Circe was a demoness who turned men into pigs," Fred said. "Did she read books too? Maybe have a sex change?"

"Men don't have to have a spell on them to turn into pigs," Cordy said acidly. "Some of them can do it all by themselves."

Momentarily distracted, Lorne and Gunn gave her injured glances.

Angel was staring at their unwilling guest, listening to the increase in his heart rate, and his breathing. It wasn't Lorne he was responding to; nor was it the mention of Lilah, because Wes had mentioned that they'd seen Lilah at the club. That left—

Cordelia, walking behind the chairs, yelped, tripping over a chair leg as a vision hit her.

Angel caught her before she hit the floor, noting as he moved that Gunn was blocking O'Flaherty. O'Flaherty, however, was no longer making any attempt to get away.

He didn't give a damn at the moment about O'Flaherty. Cordelia was holding her head in her hands to help herself concentrate, and was talking as fast as she could. "Wes! It's Wesley, I can see him, and oh god there's a *thing*, a . . . I don't know what it is, it's huge . . . it's . . . I see pages."

"Cordy, where is he? *Where is he?*"

"I can't tell! I can't see! I can see him trying to run, knocking things down to try to slow it down, he doesn't have any weapons, there are other people there and the thing, it's, oh, it's *eating* somebody—" She gagged. "And the pages—it's all pages, all around him, I can't see anything but paper, the paper's all bloody, he's—"

"Oh, bloody hell. He's in a book," O'Flaherty said from across the room.

As he spoke, Cordelia moaned in relief and sagged in Angel's arms. "Oh, thank heavens. That's it."

"He's what?" Gunn said. "What d'you mean, 'in a book'?"

Cordy took a couple of deep, careful breaths, making sure the vision was really gone, and let Angel help her back to her feet. "Yeah," she said, wonderingly. "I think he's right. The pages, and everything. It sounds crazy, but it feels right."

"How can you be in a book?" said Gunn. "And how can we get him out if he's in one? And how are we supposed to be able to find out when Wes is the one—"

Angel cut him off, turning to O'Flaherty. "I think our guest is going to help us, aren't you, Mr. O'Flaherty?"

O'Flaherty took a deep breath. "Oh, call me Adrian, won't you? It will make things so much easier."

"Do you know what Cordy's talking about?"

"Not exactly," he admitted. "But"—he traded Angel stare for stare—"it looks like my interests run with yours after all. I'm not certain about the book. I know of one that it *might* be, but . . . do you know of any Izzaret demons in this city of yours? They're collectors. Compulsive. I've been looking for them but haven't been able to locate any. They'd be able to tell you more, I think."

"Do you know any spells for pulling people out of books?" Gunn challenged him.

"Not a one. I'm not sure there is such a thing. We'd need to ask an Izzaret—assuming you can find one that collects books, and not feathers, or seashells, or Mardi Gras beads, or outdated Tube maps."

"And get a move on," Cordelia said sharply. "Unless somebody else has a better idea. Because that thing looked really, really hungry, and it was aiming right for Wes."

All his life he has heard stories about vampires— the demons who inhabited this world, who took over human bodies, who feasted on human blood. He knows that most people consider them myths, subjects fit only for horror movies and fairy tales. He has always felt secretly—perhaps not so secretly—superior to those ordinary people who don't know the terrible reality of the world they live in, the world in which they are the prey of the undead, in which they are defended by one Chosen One in a generation, and there is a secret Council that has existed for centuries, sworn to train and groom the Chosen One's potential successors.

He has read about demons and vampires and Slayers and Watchers, studied them for years. He knows the histories of the most dreaded vampires and the most heroic Slayers. He has read the Chronicles of the Watchers, determined that if training is the key to activating a Slayer, then the potential Slayer that he is assigned to will be the best-trained girl the Council has ever seen; for he has no doubt that his destiny is to be an Active Watcher one day.

Every student at the Academy knows the name of the current Active Watcher. Karrens is not that Watcher. So she has been assigned to a Slayer-in-Waiting. Why is she here?

The name is familiar, though. Father had said something. He tries to remember. He tries very hard to remember, because it gives him something to focus on besides the reality in front of him.

He has never seen a vampire in the flesh before. Part of his mind notes the characteristic hyper-developed supraorbital ridges, the broadened brow, the yellow, glowing eyes, and, of course, the fangs. One cannot miss the fangs. The mouth is parted somewhat, as if it is impossible to close the lips over the array of sharp, arched dentition. Or perhaps the thing is smiling. If it was not wearing its demonic aspect, it would probably be a rather pleasant-looking young woman, with neatly braided brown hair hanging to her waist, wearing *jeans, sensible hiking shoes, and a jeans jacket. Its hands are tucked into the jacket pockets. Very casual. Very relaxed. Smiling. Mouth gaping.*

He is afraid that if he looks at it, and it looks back at him, he will lose control of his bladder. His heart is hammering. He can hear a keening noise, a whine of terror, and he is praying that it is not coming from him.

What was it Father had said: Inadequate, not fit to carry on his name . . .

The woman facing the demon on the floor of the Testing Room, Gillie Karrens, had been a field Watcher less than three months ago. The news had swept the lunchroom and the dormitories: "The Slayer is dead; another's been Called. A girl in Australia this time—" And all the interest had shifted at once to the new Slayer, the new Active Watcher. He had wanted to know how the Slayer had died, of course, in order to teach his future student how to avoid the same mistake. He had asked Father.

Father had said something instead about a Watcher who had lost a potential. Sent her out and gotten her killed. Set her up to take a risk she wouldn't take herself. Yes. That was Karrens. He hadn't paid enough attention to that, because of course it was a mistake he would never make. Could not imagine making.

And now here she is. Standing. Unarmed.

Facing a vampire.

The vampire has been physically restrained in some fashion, but the restraints are gone now. It looks up at the circle of students staring down, its yellow gaze meeting theirs, and it laughs. He thinks he can smell the copper-tainted foulness even from where he stands. He is clutching the railing with both hands, thinking, It can reach me if it wants to. It can kill me. I could die here. *He is sick with fear, and his gaze slides away from that of the creature before it can freeze him where he stands, and it rests on Karrens—Karrens, who is standing less than thirty feet from the thing, her hands empty and open at her sides, utterly helpless.*

"Please feel free to render any assistance you feel advisable," Madame Shearer had said.

CHAPTER TWELVE

The Wyrm was perhaps fifty feet away, swinging the forward half of its body as it came to knock a path through the forest of pages. All around, Wesley could hear voices, screaming at him to move, *move,* hide, get out of the way. Gabriel yanked at his arm and was gone.

The voices grew more insistent, and the Wyrm slowed, its antennae trying to point at all the voices at once. By that time Wesley was moving, too, trying to put as many of the pages as possible between himself and the monster.

The Wyrm screamed in frustration and rose up, nearly two thirds of its body balanced on the last pair of legs. Wesley dropped flat, his heart beating so loudly, he was certain the thing hunting him surely must hear it.

The voices came from every direction, it seemed. He could hear both men and women calling, one gibe on top of the next, from every point of the compass.

The Wyrm screamed again and twisted in place.

Wesley stared at the papers his fingers were digging into. He couldn't help but read the words under his hands, automatically translating the ancient Akkadian characters: *The demons gather each year at the hill of the Golden King, and the priests make great sacrifices; but the King does not sacrifice; the King sacrifices alone—*

My word, he thought, *that's exactly what old Twizham Major claimed, but he could never find the sources to back him up. . . .*

The Wyrm was shrieking again, but it was following the voices now, not him.

Not him.

When O'Flaherty found him again, he was on his hands and knees, searching for a missing page of Akkadian history.

"Izzaret?" Angel said thoughtfully. "Lorne?"

"Don't look at me, creampie. Unless it's a music collector, in which case I might know somebody who knows somebody who knows a little bird. Now that would be an Izzaret for my tastes. But probably not," the Pylean added hastily, off Angel's exasperated look.

"Gunn?"

Gunn shrugged. "I'm more into clubbing 'em

than asking about their hobbies," he said. "I'm guessing these Izzaret guys are in the 'mean, ugly and not human' category? My club was a two-by, not a taking-roll and social-hour." He glanced at Lorne, who was giving him a wide-bloodred-eyed hurt look. "Hey, bro, you ain't mean."

"*And?*" the demon asked pointedly.

Gunn rolled his eyes. "Okay. Gorgeously green, but damn, you still ain't human."

"Should *hope* not," he said, smoothing shiny lapels and inspecting clawed fingernails.

"Look, can we knock it off here?" Angel snapped. "I'm trying to remember. I know I've seen an Izzaret in this town, and it had something to do with books. Wesley would know. . . ."

"Wesley's kind of the subject of the inquiry," Fred pointed out, in completely unnecessary fashion. "Well, he *is*," she protested, as they all shook their heads. "Maybe it had something to do with some of his own books?"

Adrian O'Flaherty laughed softly, a wry sound with as much bitterness as amusement. "We're all cursed with books," he said. "I think it's in our genes. Or one of the requirements to be a Watcher. If Pryce found an Izzaret in this city, it was a book collector, for certain."

"I've got it," Angel said abruptly. "That place just above Mulholland, in those hills just west of Universal City. Gunn, you remember? Here's what we're going to do. Gunn, you and Fred head for Lilah's. See if you can find any old red books lying around. It's a long shot, but she might have taken some of the stuff home, and it's easier than trying her office. Lorne, you and Cordy stay here and hold the fort. O'Flaherty, you and I are going to visit a demon."

"This is the same area the auction was held in," O'Flaherty observed as they followed a winding road above Mulholland Drive. "Are we going back to the Egan place?"

Angel snorted. "Not likely. This is a lower-rent set of hills. These guys only get their kids new cars once or twice a year. And then only Porsches."

He swung the convertible around a tight curve, into a cul-de-sac, and pulled up in front of a modest driveway bordered by trees and bushes. "Here we go." He hopped out without bothering to open the door.

O'Flaherty took a more conventional method, looking around as he shut the car door. There were no vehicles parked on the street; only two other driveways were visible in the circular area. The one car he could see was, in fact, a Porsche.

"Are you coming?" Angel was halfway up the drive. O'Flaherty hurried to catch up.

"So you've been here before? You know this demon?"

"Not exactly," Angel admitted. "I know he lives here, because I brought Wesley here a while back to pick up something. But I didn't go in, so I haven't actually met the guy. I figure that gives me the element of surprise."

O'Flaherty shook his head. "Surprise. Yes."

"You know, you sound an awful lot like Wes. And Giles, too. You know Giles?"

"We've met," O'Flaherty said cautiously.

"Do they teach you to sound like that in Watcher school?"

"Do they teach you to behave like this in vampire school?" O'Flaherty snapped back at him, and then stopped, aghast.

Angel stopped too, and stared at him, startled. "Excuse me?" He could hear the man's heart suddenly thundering, the smell of panic rich in the air.

The Watcher licked suddenly dry lips. "I— sorry." He took a deep breath and squared his shoulders. "This is . . . rather odd . . . and you seem to take it in somewhat antic fashion. When I came to Los Angeles, I didn't expect to be driving about alone at night with . . . you."

Angel studied him. O'Flaherty's breathing had steadied, and his pulse, while still fast, wasn't quite as wild as a moment before. But he could still see it throbbing, teasing, in the man's throat.

And O'Flaherty could see him seeing it.

At Watchers school they'd been taught about

that worst of all vampires, Angelus. His fists were knotted at his sides.

Angel sighed. "Well, here we are. I'm sorry I'm not living down to your education. Or rather, I'm not sorry. Right now, we've got things to do and demons to see. Can we deal with your Great Expectations after we rescue Wesley?"

"Yes, of course." O'Flaherty swallowed again, and unclenched his hands. "The Izzaret."

They proceeded up the driveway to the white stucco, traditional-style house without further discussion and rang the doorbell, to all appearances nothing more than two young men calling upon an acquaintance.

"I might live down to a few of them," Angel picked up the thread of conversation again casually, as they waited for someone to answer the door, "if we don't get some answers. I'm kinda looking forward to taking things out on someone. Not you," he added hastily.

"Of course not," O'Flaherty said, keeping his gaze straight ahead.

They could hear a thumping and dragging on the other side of the door, as if someone, or something, was making its way with some difficulty to respond to the summons of the doorbell. Finally the door swung open.

"*Skeeat-ik?*"

The two of them jumped, and looked down to

see a small purple-knobbly-skinned demon standing approximately knee-high before them. It was looking up at them, three-fingered fists planted firmly on its hips.

"Hi," Angel said. "Are you Dabet?"

"Skeeat-ik!tokat?"

"We're looking for an Izzaret demon named Dabet. Would that be you?"

"Tik shissthissa !istsss misrtistik!" Outraged demon saliva sprayed in their direction.

"I beg your pardon," O'Flaherty said smoothly. "You're quite right, it *is* late to be calling. We apologize."

"You speak Izzaret?" Angel asked him sharply.

The little demon hissed and clicked at them some more, and kicked Angel in the shins.

O'Flaherty ignored the vampire hopping on one foot beside him. "We came because we wanted to ask you about a particular, special book," he said. "We've heard that you know more about books than anyone in California. May we come in?"

More sputters from the Izzaret.

"Actually, we're interested in buying at the moment. But we might have something to sell in future, if you were interested. Right now, though—"

The little demon cocked his head to one side, studying the two of them. Angel was leaning over, rubbing his leg. "Why'd he kick me?" he demanded.

"Izzarets don't like what they consider silly questions," O'Flaherty said. "I wasn't *speaking* Izzaret. Izzaret is a very difficult language, highly nuanced, with a number of delicate—"

The little demon kicked O'Flaherty in the shins.

"Let me guess," Angel said. "Izzarets don't like flattery, either."

"Er, yes."

"I think I like this guy."

The Izzaret waved them into its house.

The geas that kept vampires from entering a home uninvited lifted its hold on Angel, and he followed the little demon inside, with O'Flaherty close behind.

"Oh my," Angel said under his breath. It seemed like a totally inadequate reaction.

The walls of the entryway were lined with bookcases. These shelves had none of the fussy neatness of a library. Books were double-stacked, lying on their sides, wedged tight; more books were stacked on top of the cases to the ceiling. The little Izzaret probably found the gap between the shelves adequate for its needs; the two full-grown men were tempted to slide sideways between the looming books. Glimpsing into the kitchen as they passed, they saw it similarly packed. Only the stovetop was innocent of books.

The demon led the two of them down the hall into the living room—or what was probably originally intended to be a living room—where they found still more bookshelves lining the walls, and books stacked on the floor around three very small, overstuffed leather chairs, gathered in front of a pleasantly crackling fireplace. A tiny table next to one of the chairs held a mug of something aromatic and steaming. A low table in front of the other two chairs was buried in more books and magazines and what appeared to be computer printouts.

When they looked up, instead of the ceiling, they saw . . . more books.

From the outside the house had appeared to be a one-story, traditional house. There wasn't even a room over the garage. But this room had all the appearance of a multistory library tower.

"Excuse me," O'Flaherty said, "have we stepped into a police call box?"

"!KSksrik!li tik tik likeke qu!ivivrikSkisksikrlik."

"I'm sorry. Of course. We're being invited to sit down," he told Angel. The two of them looked around. "I think it had better be on the floor," he added unnecessarily.

They shifted piles of books, carefully, and Angel took a look at some of the titles. "Russian history? You know that Anastasia died in nineteen seventeen, right? That woman in Virginia was a Polish imposter."

"Kshrov tok veris ! ! kzi."

Angel looked to O'Flaherty, who knitted his brows a bit uncertainly. "I'm not sure. Dimensional allohistory?"

Angel looked blank. "Dimensional what?"

The little demon spat and crackled some more.

"Alternate universes, basically," O'Flaherty said. "He says they're about alternate histories in different dimensions."

Angel shrugged. "I guess. Ask him about the book. Our book. The one we came about."

O'Flaherty nodded.

The next part of the conversation was completely incomprehensible to the vampire. Suddenly Dabet nearly leaped off the chair and into O'Flaherty's lap, screaming at him. Taken aback, O'Flaherty said, "Well, I didn't really see the thing, but apparently it *was* a red book, as a matter of fact." He turned to Angel. "Yes, he knows about the book."

"I can see that," Angel said dryly. "So why is he so excited about it? And why is Wolfram and Hart so interested in it? And, more to the point, what does he know about where Wes has gone?"

Listening to the next exchange, he tried to pick out names and words, but it was impossible to isolate them from the series of clicks and tones, like a bizarre hybrid of Chinese and Kalahari. At one point O'Flaherty fell suddenly silent, and then said something back to the little demon, slowly.

Dabet repeated himself, and sat with his purple tongue licking in and out, nictating membranes flicking sideways across his eyes. Angel got the impression that this was the Izzaret version of uproarious laughter, although he couldn't say why. O'Flaherty, however, was definitely not laughing.

"You're absolutely certain of that," he said at last.

Dabet repeated himself yet again.

"Thank you," O'Flaherty said, very formally, and he added something in Izzaret. Dabet's tongue-licking and eye-flicking ceased, and he nodded solemnly in return.

Angel felt as if he had just been left out of something important, and he didn't like it. "What's the deal?" he snapped. "What's going on?"

O'Flaherty took a deep breath and turned to him as if slightly surprised to be reminded of his existence—another thing that the vampire didn't much like.

"The book. Yes. Dabet knows about the book, and he thinks he knows what happened to Wesley too. The problem appears to be quite a bit worse than we thought. It's not simply a case of evil lawyers breaking into Wyndam-Pryce's apartment and stealing a book from him. This particular book, as I told you already, is notorious in occult lore. Our friend Dabet here had suspected it might turn up in the Gilman auction, simply because so many powerful individuals were going to attend. The fact that someone like Wesley is missing in association with a book from that auction merely confirms it."

"Will you get to the *point*," Angel said.

"Very well. This book, which is currently in the hands of your friends at Wolfram and Hart, has in all probability eaten Wesley Wyndam-Pryce. Dabet says that he's most likely been turned into nothing more than—printed words by this time."

"He's been *what*?" Angel looked from O'Flaherty to the Izzaret and back again, and then, uneasily, up and around at the shelves of volumes towering over them. "Are you nuts?"

"The book is the creation of a demon that has come to be called the Bookwyrm. It seeks out magicians, sorcerers, occult researchers—human ones, not demonic. Really, it's a remarkable case of magickal entrapment. It's in the form its prey will find most attractive—as a book, naturally—and when the person reads it, the Wyrm snatches him or her inside and devours them. The person's substance is then written into the book, which simply makes it more attractive to the next victim."

Angel was convinced the book was awful; he wanted to cut to the chase. "How do we get him out?"

"Well . . ." O'Flaherty hesitated, and then turned back to Dabet. Much hissing and clicking ensued. Finally he turned back to Angel, while the tiny demon hopped down from his leather chair and scampered out of the room. "He says he's not sure there's any point in trying, but he's willing to work with me to give it a shot."

"And what does he want in return?" There was no such thing as a free lunch, or a demonic favor.

"He'd like to have the book, of course."

"He's not afraid of this Worm, I take it?"

"Wyrm." O'Flaherty gave the word a subtly different pitch. "And no, he isn't. I think he must be immune to it or something. But he says that we need to get together with the book in a quiet place pretty soon, because if it isn't already too late, it will be. He doesn't know how long it takes for the Wyrm to write off its victims, but he doesn't think it would take too long."

"He can't do it by himself? He can't tell you how to do it by yourself?"

"No. It's going to take both of us. If I tried to do it by myself, I'd get pulled in by the Wyrm the same way Wesley was. And apparently Dabet can't do it by himself."

At this point Dabet re-entered the room and climbed back into the chair, rubbing its little purple hands against the fabric of its trousers. At least, Angel was reasonably sure it was fabric; the material was the same color as the demon's skin. There was a chance, he supposed, that it was just more of Dabet.

"Why'd he leave?" Angel wanted to know.

"Even demons have to visit the WC once in a while," O'Flaherty said uncomfortably. "Besides, I think he wanted to give us a couple of minutes to talk."

Dabet erupted in another susurrus of hissing.

"He also says," O'Flaherty translated, "that if it's true that the book has been obtained by Wolfram and Hart—"

"You just had to tell him the whole story, didn't you?" Angel muttered.

"It does help to have full information."

"Yeah, I've noticed you're the full-disclosure kinda guy. A real presidential candidate."

Tsk!tik! Dabet interrupted the glaring match.

O'Flaherty expelled a long breath. "If it's true that the book has been obtained by Wolfram and Hart," he repeated, "then they did so to try to read it into Files and Records as well as enter it into their Special Collections." His voice dropped on the last two words, became positively icy. Angel noted the fact with interest. O'Flaherty didn't explain why he was so averse to one particular branch of Wolfram & Hart. Special Collections? He'd said his father was a librarian. . . .

"So what happens to Wes if they do that?"

"Dabet isn't sure, but if he hasn't already been written into the book by the Wyrm, he's fairly sure that being read into Files and Records will at least kill him. It will certainly drive him mad. If he isn't already."

"Then I guess it's time to check in with Fred and Gunn," Angel said grimly, and reached into a pocket for his cell phone.

"Um, I don't think that's going to work in here," Dabet said in perfectly clear English. "Modern technology and magickal libraries just don't mix very well."

"Thanks so much," Angel replied after a long pause. "I'll just step outside, then."

"Although," he heard the little demon say as he stepped out the door, "I've got a very nice set of programs on my computer that makes keeping track of acquisitions and sales *so* much easier than it was a hundred years ago—"

"My father used to say the same thing," O'Flaherty was agreeing as the door swung closed.

Lilah Morgan hated bringing work home. Well, there were certain exceptions, such as Wesley Wyndam-Pryce, but for the most part she definitely did not want anything associated with Wolfram & Hart in her apartment.

Wanting, of course, was not the same as having, and a lawyer's work was never done. She brought work home almost every night, and stayed up late reviewing briefs, arguments, and her latest personal campaign for position and favor with the senior partners. She'd done so ever since signing on as the most junior associate with the firm. It wasn't that she didn't enjoy her work; it was just that sometimes, every once in a while, she thought it might be nice to have one tiny corner of her life that was almost . . . normal.

If only she could remember what normal was.

On the other hand, she was fairly sure that normal didn't pay nearly as well as her day job.

Just now, however, what she had brought home was both not normal, and not work. At least not work yet. She was simply confirming that the volume that her staff had obtained for her, at the request of the head of the Special Collections, really was the volume in question. That was going to be her story, and she was sticking to it, at least until she found a better one.

And she had brought a former member of the Special Collections staff who happened to owe her some favors—big ones, involving leaving the firm without having to die first—here to her own home, just to find out.

And she had her mother here to test the theory on, if her mother would only keep *still*—

"Lilah, darling, are you sure this isn't too big a place for you? It's very nice, but the rent must be very high." Mrs. Morgan was dressed in a simple, inexpensive rose cotton day dress with a matching sweater. Her daughter had inherited her high cheekbones, thick hair, fine expressive eyes, and slender stature; Lilah got her height from her father. Even before the osteoporosis had kicked in, her mother had barely come to her shoulder.

Mrs. Morgan darted from one side of the room to the other, lightly touching the table, the china cabinet, the frame of a picture. She moved like a hummingbird, never pausing long, always freezing in place for just long enough to look and then flickering away again. Lilah caught her just before she headed back to the bedrooms. Her feet scuffed in her slippers against the hardwood floors.

"That's all right, Mother, I can afford it." She took the older woman by the hand and led her back to the chair inside the protective circle painted on the paneled floor. And wasn't *that* going to be hell to get out of the wood when all this was over with? But it would be worth it if this actually worked.

"I suppose if you have roommates. But how many bedrooms did you say there were?" The older woman got up again and started toward the back of the apartment again. "The rent must be very high here."

The Izzaret seated in the high chair in the middle of the pentagram, holding the age-blackened "red" book balanced precariously in its lap, shoved an oversized pair of spectacles up on a purple snub nose and gave Lilah an exasperated glance.

"I won't be held responsible for what happens to

her," it said for the fourth or fifth time. "If she keeps on breaking the protective wards, there's no telling what could come out."

"I *know* that," Lilah said through gritted teeth, and pursued her mother into her bedroom, where she found her standing beside the bed with a pair of handcuffs in her hand and a bemused look on her face.

"Ah, Mother—"

"Are we at your aunt Sophie's?" Mrs. Morgan asked, holding out the metal bracelets to her daughter. "Sophie was looking for these the other day."

"I don't think so, Mom." She took the handcuffs from her mother's hands and slipped them into the nightstand drawer—it was partly open; what *else* had she found in there? Maybe her mind was so foggy, she didn't recognize . . . "Why don't we go into the other room and sit down and have a cup of tea, all right?"

Her mother's eyebrows furrowed together, and her soft eyes grew worried and confused. "I don't like that little boy in there," she said. "I don't want to go in there, Lilah. He frightens me."

"It's all right, Mother." She took her mother's hands—when did the skin become so cool and thin? When did those brown spots start to appear?—in both of hers, and started to draw her toward the door. "Come on. We'll just sit down for a little while. He isn't going to hurt you. And then you'll feel lots better! Just for a little while, I promise. Come on, Mother."

But the older woman continued to protest. "No, I don't want to go. No! I don't want to go! No. No. No! *No! No! No! No!*" She tried to jerk her hands away, out of her daughter's grasp, and Lilah's hands automatically tightened.

"Mother, *stop it!*" For one instant she almost slapped the frantically screaming older woman. Instead, she let her go, and watched as her mother crawled weeping onto the bed and up to the headboard, curling up as far away from her as she could get, sniffling and peeking at her from under one pink-cardigan arm.

She couldn't understand it. She had no problems beheading a rival at work; she could flay an enemy without turning a hair. But now, looking at her mother huddled fearfully on her bed, all she felt was helplessness.

"Filial piety," said the little Izzaret from the doorway. "It crops up in the oddest places. You humans really do amaze me sometimes."

Mrs. Morgan, seeing the Izzaret, had started screaming and thrashing again, and was wadding the satin coverlet into a knotted mess. Lilah counted to ten. That coverlet had been part of a six-thousand-dollar set, and she had already had it dry-cleaned once this week.

"Imgishafu, I suggest you get back to work," she said evenly. "We'll be out in a minute, and I expect you to have that spell ready to go. Are we clear on this?"

"Absolutely, Ms. Morgan." Imgishafu scampered back into the living room and started chanting again. Mrs. Morgan's screaming promptly died away as soon as he was out of sight.

Lilah made a wide circle around her mother and went into the bathroom to open the narcotics safe. Filial piety was all very well, but special circumstances were called for. One way or another, her mother was going to sit in that chair in the middle of that circle while a spell was cast on her.

She hoped she had something for her mother to wear while the demon was doing it.

CHAPTER THIRTEEN

"Have you thought about trying to follow the thing? Keep track of its movements?" Wesley suggested.

It was some time later—how long, he had no idea. Gabriel O'Flaherty had collected two more of the Wyrm's victims from the diversion team, and now they were busy trying to educate Wesley about the realities of the book. Their realities seemed to be thoroughly pessimistic. So much so, in fact, that the others who had participated in distracting the thing from him hadn't even bothered to show up to be introduced. Wesley could see why Gabriel wasn't sure exactly how many living people were in the book.

The other three gave him a pitying look, not the first they had sent his way since they had started this discussion. "We've thought of that, you know," said one of them. His name was Michael Blanton, and he was a Canadian thaumaturge who had last been heard from in the 1920s. He was chubby and red-faced, and his thin blond hairline was in full flight from his thin blond eyebrows. Wesley had run across his name as the author of some not-very-good studies of Madame Blatavsky, but had otherwise never heard of him. He wouldn't have remembered that much if Blanton hadn't introduced himself as a renowned authority on the subject. "We've been here a while. Thought of it all, chap. That's how we've stayed alive, don't you know."

The fake British accent grated on his nerves. At any moment Wesley expected the man to whip out a cricket bat and proclaim that his name was Earnest, don't you know. As it was, the man sounded about as British as—well, as Cordelia.

"The Wyrm doesn't stay corporeal," a rather pudgy, short-haired woman named Matterdorf amplified. "Can't track it. It appears, attacks, digests, writes, and, having writ, moves on." She appeared rather too pleased with her witticism. She also appeared rather too wide-eyed at the sight of Wesley, and tried rather too hard to stand in his line of sight. It made him distinctly uncomfortable, especially when he noted her flared nostrils and deep breathing. He was familiar with the notion of men undressing women with their eyes, but had never experienced the phenomenon aimed at himself. At least, not in a public place.

Besides, she was at least twenty years older than he was. He had read her treatise on the roots of Nazi occultism just before the Council had sent him to Sunnydale and had thought it fascinating—even considered writing her a fan letter about it. Now he was glad he hadn't. "How do you guard against it, then?" he asked.

"You can't, old man. Have to be prepared to fight at all times. Always on your guard. On your toes!"

Wesley wondered who the man was trying to impress—him as the latest addition to their group, or Matterdorf, or perhaps just himself?

"It likes to rush," Matterdorf said, diverted from Wesley long enough to send a glower at Blanton. "Generally from just out of sight. So we try to stay in clear areas as much as we can, and we listen."

"For the noise of its coming," O'Flaherty the elder put in. "You heard it yourself, when it took Artie."

"Oh, it got Artie? Bad show!" Blanton planted a hammy fist into the other meaty palm. "It'll pay for that, it will."

Blanton, Wesley decided, had seen one too many World War I music-hall revues. Or perhaps a dozen too many. And perhaps too much Gilbert and Sullivan as well.

"And *how* do you fight it?" he asked Blanton acidly.

The three of them looked at one another, suddenly wary.

"After all, if you intend to make the Wyrm pay for taking Artie, presumably you have a way of doing so. Don't you?"

Blanton turned bright red and sputtered.

"It's as I told you," O'Flaherty said. "You run. Try to put a lot of clear text between yourself and it if you can. That seems to slow it down. It will go through the pages, reading."

"It reads?"

"Certainly it reads. It writes, doesn't it?" For Matterdorf, the two things were inseparable. "It likes to review whom it's eaten, I think. Chewing the verbal cud, you see. Or it would be, if it were a cow."

Which it was not. The suggestion started a train of thought in Wesley's mind.

"Once, Ali ibn Idris set up a trap for it, they say," Blanton said, the annoying mannerisms abruptly gone. The change in manner derailed Wes's train of thought completely. "He lured it into a tunnel, and collapsed a whole library's worth of manuscripts on top of the thing. Tons of them."

"What happened?"

Blanton shrugged, another red flush flooding through his fair skin. "It ate its way out. Took ibn Idris, too." He reached into a pocket, pulled out a piece of paper, smoothed it out, and showed it to him. Wesley blinked, mentally shifting gears to follow the elegant Arabic calligraphy from right to

241

left across the page: *In the Name of the Compassionate and the Most Merciful! I, Ali, note these things. In the matter of the Iblis of the second dimension, accursed be its name . . .*

Ali ibn Idris—a pen name for a medieval Arabic sorcerer. He had studied the man's works in the third year at the Academy, translated the elegant, poetic text as a part of his final examination.

Ali ibn Idris had been alive all this time. Here. If he'd found the book earlier, he might have actually met him, spoken to him, asked what he had really meant in some of those difficult passages.

He wondered who else he had studied might actually still be alive in the book, and how many he had just missed. How many of his early heroes had been mercilessly devoured as he had seen Artie devoured?

"'Mother'?" Fred whispered. "That's her *mom*?"

"I didn't know she had a mother," Gunn muttered. "I thought she was hatched. Or crawled out from under a rock somewhere."

"Oh, definitely hatched. She's too pretty to have crawled out from under a rock."

Gunn looked at Lilah—tall, elegant, stylish, perfectly groomed—and then at Fred—gawky, coltish, still unsure of herself on pretty much anything except the hard sciences. He shrugged. He knew which one he preferred.

The two of them were crouched on the balcony

of the apartment, on either side of the sliding-glass door. Lilah had left the curtains open, and they could see her wrestling a sleepy? drunken? drugged? older woman into a straight-backed chair, and had picked up the word "Mother." The lawyer was far too distracted to hear the low-toned conversation taking place on the other side of the closed glass door fifteen feet away.

As for the small purple demon sitting in the child's high chair, with an open book on the tray in front of him, he was too wrapped up in an evocation chant to bother with anything at all going on around him.

"What's she doing?" Fred said.

"Damned if I know," Gunn answered. "Looks like she's trying to cast a spell on her or something."

"On her own *mother*?" Fred squawked, outraged.

Lilah's head came around sharply. She paused, as if thinking about going over to the door, but instead went over to the telephone lying on the counter, picked it up, and hit a single button. "Wellington? This is Lilah Morgan. Run a security team by my apartment. Now. I think I may have some Peeping Toms. . . . All-night coverage. It'll be excellent practice for them." Snapping the phone shut, she smiled thinly, crossed the room to the glass door, and firmly closed the curtains.

"Well, that tears it," Gunn said. "We'd better get out of here before the heavies show up."

"I'm sorry," Fred said as they slipped from the balcony and back to the street where they had left the car. "But—casting spells on her own mother! That's just awful!"

"That's just Lilah," her companion pointed out. "She's evilness."

"Do you think she's got that book in there?"

"It's not like we could have gotten in there tonight, anyway," Gunn said consolingly. He started the car and pulled out into the light traffic leading into the freeway on-ramp. "Not with her right there, and her mom, and that little demon guy and all. And who knows who else in back. We're not exactly sure what we're looking for, so we can't just barge in and hold them at gunpoint and take what we want. Besides, trying that with a lawyer is just never a good way to start the day."

"But we really need to get it. It's important. We should go back," Fred insisted.

Gunn glanced over at her. "Are you crazy? She heard you. She was calling out the troops. We go back, we get our asses nailed. Probably end up in jail—if not worse."

Fred knew a logical argument when she heard one, but she didn't have to like it. "O'Flaherty said that Wes was *in* the book—what did he mean by that?"

"Got no idea. I figure we go back, report in, and come up with a new idea. And maybe we can find out."

• • •

Emilio limped into the kitchen, opened the refrigerator, and took out a carton of milk. His leg was still hot, but it didn't hurt, exactly. He could still move pretty good. It looked funny, but that was okay. The marks on his leg were all different colors now, and his fingers felt funny too. They were changing colors at the tips, red-orange, like the little demons, and little drips kept forming under his nails. He wiped them on his shirt.

His little sister was packing up her books from studying at the kitchen table again.

"Where's Dad?" he asked.

His sister shrugged. "Working, I guess. He hasn't been home."

Emilio finished off the milk, drinking directly from the carton, and considered. So, not home yet? "Where's Mom?"

Another shrug.

Emilio tossed the carton into the trash and walked out.

His father's office was usually locked, but the spell that had let him into Cawber's worked just as well here. He'd been in here before, and he was familiar with the shelves of legal books; the filing cabinet full of papers; the computer, sitting dark, on the cheap table his father used for a desk.

His books weren't anywhere to be found.

He checked over the shelves carefully, but his

books looked nothing like the reference books his father had.

He must have taken them to work, like he said.

Emilio closed his eyes at the rush of pure rage, grabbing on to the back of the swivel chair to hold himself up. How dare he take those books. How *dare* he. Those books belonged to *him*, Emilio, and he had no *right* to just walk in and take them. Those books were his, his power, those books made him *important*.

And he wanted them back.

The Buick was gone?

Fine. He'd take the bus.

"Who is that?" Matterdorf said. They were watching a well-groomed man look around, bewildered, at his surroundings. They'd been moving at random across the landscape—it was all the same, really, no Exit signs anywhere—when the man had popped into place not far ahead of them, in a clear space among the pages.

"I recognize him. That's one of the thugs who works for Lilah Morgan."

"Who's she?" There was a distinct trace of jealousy in the dumpy woman's voice. *Spare me,* Wesley thought. He wondered why his companions didn't go out to greet the newcomer. He decided to follow their lead. They'd stayed alive this long; they must have a good reason.

Blanton's and Gabriel O'Flaherty's initial reaction to the appearance of a stranger was to hang back and wait. Matterdorf looked as if she was less certain—it was a good-looking young man, after all. Bowing to the older men's experience, Wes stayed back with them. This was what he'd felt when he first fell into the book, this sensation of being watched; it was interesting to be the watcher. Not, he thought, "for a change." He smiled grimly to himself.

The newcomer was staring around himself, as disoriented as Wesley himself had been. He was young, in his mid-twenties at most, dressed in a conservative dark suit and white shirt with real cuffs and gold cuff links, and a silk tie that probably cost more than Wes had seen in the past three months.

"Thuggee pays better than it used to," Blanton observed.

"Only if you're a lawyer."

"I see."

Abruptly, Gabriel clutched at Wesley's arm and pulled him into a grove of scrolls. He held a finger to his lips, signaling silence, and then pointed frantically back behind the newcomer. Blanton followed. After a moment, so did Matterdorf, scrambling clumsily after them.

At first Wesley couldn't see anything other than the piles of paper and scrolls that made up the landscape of this strange place. Then he heard a faint sighing sound, as if air had been displaced.

Then a scratching, much as a badly sharpened quill might make on rough material. Or clawed feet, scratching, as they pulled a heavy body on a hesitant journey.

Gabriel saw it first, and his fingers bit into the muscles of Wesley's forearm. Then Wesley saw it too: the too-familiar massive triangular silver-gray head rising above the pages, swimming back and forth on an elongated stalk of a body, blindly seeking.

The Wyrm.

The newcomer hadn't seen the demon yet. Wesley drew breath to call out a warning, but Gabriel shook his head frantically; as he did so, the huge head swung blindly in their direction, almost as if the thing was sniffing for them, its antennae writhing, stretching out, making thin whistling noises as they lashed the air. It had lifted perhaps the first third of its body straight up, balancing it as it crawled.

Toward them.

"Too close," Gabriel breathed in his ear. He pulled Wesley back.

It was the sound of the antennae whipping through the air that finally attracted the lawyer's attention. He had been examining one of the smaller stacks of paper, pulling off several pages and reading them intently. The Wyrm was moving at an angle away from him, toward the grove of papyrus scrolls, toward Wesley and the others, when he looked up and saw the huge body perhaps thirty feet away, a flattened cylinder thicker than he was tall even before the demon raised itself up to search.

The man screamed.

The Wyrm paused, its antennae still frantically lashing, and its jaws parted as it tilted its head in almost comical bemusement. A line of clear drool escaped from one glistening fang.

The lawyer dropped the pages and scrambled backward, tripping over the pile of manuscript he'd just been reading.

The Wyrm turned to the sound, and the man screamed again.

The demon attacked.

Gabriel yanked Wesley away from the sound of wet crunching, and the four of them ran.

Angel paused outside the door, the shell of the cell phone lifted but not yet open. The door to the Izzaret's magick library had closed, but not shut. The vampire listened.

Flaherty said something, a long string of fluid hisses and sharp clicks.

"While I appreciate your efforts," Dabet said, "your accent is positively excreble. We can continue in your primary human language, if you wish."

Flaherty blew out a breath of relief. "Thank you. Although I thought I was doing fairly well, all things considered."

"You were making yourself understood."

Angel smothered a chuckle and started to open the phone.

"All right," Flaherty went on, "I want him dead. Preferably by my own hand—I want to choke the life out of him myself—but I'll pay someone else if I have to.

"This is the deal: Put me in a position to kill Circe, or kill him yourself. Bring me his head, and I guarantee you'll end up with the book, with the Watcher inside."

Angel froze. His head lifted, and his features shifted, rippled, and his eyes yellowed with rage.

"Please," the little demon said. "Don't be ridiculous. Why should I take the risk of taking on a Wolfram and Hart department head on the promise of payment sometime in the future? Particularly when you don't have the wherewithal to pay? And if I put you in a position to kill him, as you put it, your chances of walking away are nonexistent. Give me the book first, and I'll see what I can arrange about putting him in your hands."

There was a silence. Angel managed to get his temper, and his demon, under control. He reached for the doorknob, then let his hand fall. So far as he knew, there was no other way out of the Library, and he wanted to hear more.

O'Flaherty sighed. "I do see your point." There

was a long pause, and then he said very softly, as if to himself, "I didn't know he worked for Wolfram and Hart. I shouldn't have been surprised, I suppose. It was a logical place for him to go. A place where I couldn't get at him."

Then he continued the conversation with Dabet: "But if you have the book, what guarantee do I have that I'll ever get a chance at him?"

"Why do you want Circe so badly, after all?" The little demon sounded genuinely curious.

"That's my business." The answer was clipped and cold.

"But you are even willing to sacrifice your friend?"

"I will sacrifice anything and anyone," O'Flaherty said. "I'm damned sorry about Wyndam-Pryce, but he's probably written into the book already, from all you've told me. Even if he wasn't, though, we were never that close."

Angel snarled softly.

"What was that?"

"I think your friend must be finished with his call," Dabet remarked. "Why don't you go join him. And when you have the book, do let me know, won't you?"

The Wyrm showed up twice more, and twice more they had tried the diversionary tactic. It worked, once; the second time, one of the nameless victims had managed to cut herself, and the Wyrm had focused on the blood, ignoring the voices. The end had been predictable, noisy, and messy.

Reading the new pages later, Wesley discovered the woman's name had been Veronika Mueller. The name wasn't familiar to him. For some reason, that made him even angrier.

"Is it vulnerable to *anything*? What have you tried against it?"

"We've tried stabbing, hitting, shooting, kicking, cutting, and screaming," Matterdorf said. Apparently Wesley's endless questions were beginning to make him a little less heartthrobby, although she and Blanton continued to stay with Gabriel and himself. Wesley resolved to ask as many more as he could think of. "None of them worked."

"Stabbing?" That sounded promising. Someone had some kind of a weapon, at least. He might be able to use that.

"David n'Goshi had a penknife on him. It ate the knife when it took David," Gabriel told him.

So much for using a weapon.

"So all you do is run away?" His frustration was beginning to show in his voice. He lowered it with effort. There was no point in attracting the Wyrm itself to their conference. "You don't try to kill it? You don't try to find a way out?"

They all looked at him, at one another.

"Our diversions work. Most of the time, anyway. If enough of us are near, and in the right place." Matterdorf was very quiet.

"We've saved a few people that way, at least," Gabriel pointed out.

"Yourself among them," Blanton pointed out.

Wesley wondered how many "a few" were, and how many, like Veronika Mueller, had been eaten in the process. He decided not to ask. The one nugget of value was that it *could* be distracted from a victim, frustrated by too many targets. That indicated a great deal about the Wyrm's ability to concentrate.

"How long does it stay gone?"

"It varies. So as soon as it disappears, we move."

"And how long have you been doing this?"

Blanton looked up at the featureless sky, as if tracking the movement of a nonexistent sun to measure a day. "Hard to tell. From what you've said, it would be, what, eighty-odd years?" He looked as if he was telling a joke. "I've made it longer in here than I would have out there, haven't I! Good show, what! I'm in grand shape for a man over a century old, amn't I!"

"*Amn't I?*" Wesley couldn't remember when he had last heard that particular construction. That, more than anything, convinced him that he really was trapped in time, in a book. That, and the nearly silent gasp from Matterdorf, standing beside him, who slipped one hand in his, will he, nill he. He wanted to thrust it away from him, but he couldn't bring himself to do it.

"Listen," she whispered. "It's coming."

Wesley wasn't sure how long they ran—long enough to get out of earshot of whatever was going on behind them, at least. When they finally stopped, he stared at Gabriel in horror. "It was coming after us," he said. "Coming straight for us."

"Coming after you, young man. I believe I told you so. Fresh blood, and all that."

"How did it know—"

"Oh, it always shows up when someone new arrives. Sooner or later. It's laid the trap, and it comes by to collect, you see." Blanton was panting, red-faced.

"It hasn't collected *you* yet—"

"Ah, but we've had the same luck you've had so far. All of us who are still alive seem to have the same story: Someone else came through shortly after and distracted the beast. Stay alive long enough, and you'll be one of us—the Wyrm will hunt you only when there isn't fresher meat available." For a dumpy woman, slow and clumsy, Matterdorf was in better condition than Blanton was. She wasn't panting nearly as hard.

"So if my friends try to rescue me—," Wesley began.

Gabriel laughed. "They probably will, but not quite as you hope. Certainly not the way they'd want to! We're all going to feed the Wyrm eventually, and get written into the book. Look there." He pointed back the way they had come.

On the horizon, not nearly far enough away, Wesley could see the Wyrm, its whole body thrashing back and forth now, rolling its entire body around; and then the demon arched high into the air, its jaws gaping wide, and a stream of dark liquid shot out of its mouth. "What is it?"

"Your thug. Or rather, everything he knows. Knew. Some of us are sure the Wyrm knows what we know as soon as we fall into the book; it doesn't fall into any traps we try to set, or any spells. But it has to eat us to write us into the book. That's what it's doing now. Writing that young man, in order to read him. If we go back there, later, we'll find everything there is to know about him."

Wesley remembered the page about Ali, and shuddered.

"Of course, whether or not it absolutely has to eat us first to know what we know," Gabriel said philosophically, "it doesn't matter as far as that young man is concerned, does it? It certainly knows it now. Of course, he was a lawyer, so that rather limited his conversation, I imagine."

"Except he worked for Wolfram and Hart," Wesley said slowly. "Did you say the Wyrm can somehow direct where the Compendium goes?"

"It does seem to, yes. Why?"

"Because I rather think that if that's the case, the next place our demon friend will want to go is a place that his latest snack knew about. If the Bookwyrm is intent on devouring knowledge, its most logical next destination is—"

"Oh, dear," Gabriel said. "Well, that does rather definitively answer the question, doesn't it? Eat first, know later. But do we really want this thing knowing everything there is to know in Wolfram and Hart's Files and Records?"

"Which includes the location of probably every above-average sorcerer in the world," Wesley completed the thought. "Every one of whom will be targeted for its next snack."

On the horizon, the Bookwyrm twisted and shuddered, moving over the pages it had just inked.

"Too late now. It's fascinated by them," Matterdorf said. "As much as any of us are. It's just that it reads so much . . . faster."

As if in agreement, the Wyrm reared up again, screaming. In triumph? Delight? The four of them watched it bloat just a little larger as it fell upon the pages once again with an obscene purr of pleasure.

And then it came to the end—they could tell by the shriek of disappointment—and it lifted itself up again, twisting around, its antennae out again, seeking.

And abruptly, it disappeared.

"Time to get moving," Blanton said. "No telling where it will pop up next."

CHAPTER FOURTEEN

"She heard something," Gunn said, "and she called in a security team. We decided we'd better get while the getting was good." He looked up as Angel and Adrian came in the door and raised a hand in greeting.

"She was casting a spell on her mom? This *was* a sweet-little-old-lady-type mom, right? Not a large-bearded, battle-ax-type?" Lorne was horrified, even as he sought to clarify their description. Lorne had issues with the whole mother thing.

"Well, not Lilah personally," Fred said. She thought about clearing up Gunn's comment about exactly why Lilah had called in that security team, and decided that if Gunn didn't want to go into details right now, she wouldn't either. Of course, with her luck it would all come out eventually. "She had this little demon guy there doing it for her. But definitely a sweet little old lady. Gray hair and everything. And it looked like she had her drugged."

"You're sure it was her mother?" Lorne was still horrified.

"Unless she's calling somebody else 'Mom,' it was."

"What kind of demon was it?" Angel asked, coming down the steps into the lobby. Adrian O'Flaherty followed just behind him.

Fred and Gunn looked at each other. Gunn shrugged. "Ugly kind?"

"It was little," Fred said. "Kind of dark. It was hard to see. It looked like it was sitting in a high chair, like for a little kid. Sorta blue, I thought, or—"

"Purple?" Angel said.

"Yeah, it could of been purple," Gunn allowed.

"Izzaret," O'Flaherty said.

"She's got one of her own," Angel agreed. "I guess that tells us she has the book, then. And there must be something in it she wants for her mother—" He broke off abruptly, silencing himself before he could add, *Wesley could probably tell us what.*

"I'm *sorry*," Fred burst out. "It's my fault! She saw me watching!"

Gunn glared at her.

Angel shook his head. "Okay," he said, "no matter what Lilah's doing, she's going to take the book in to Wolfram and Hart in the morning. We have to get it away from her before then. The only alternative is going into their offices and taking it away from them there."

There was a little silence, broken at last by Lorne. "Excuse me, creamcakes? Did I hear you right? You're officially declaring suicide?"

"Then we'll have to go back to her place tonight, security team or not," said O'Flaherty. Angel looked at him but said nothing. "Wesley is trapped inside that book. If it ends up inside Wolfram and Hart—"

"All right, all right," Lorne said hastily. "I'm convinced."

"No time like the present," Angel said dryly.

"We're going to need Dabet to get him out if we can get our hands on the book," O'Flaherty reminded him.

"Of course," Angel said. "Lorne, that will be your job. Meet us at Lilah's, but hang back until you see what's happening. The rest of us—let's get moving."

A little less than an hour later, they were back at Lilah Morgan's apartment, peering fruitlessly through windows at drawn curtains. Angel strained to hear past the breathing, heartbeats, shuffling, and movement of his team, but got nothing from the apartment.

There didn't seem to be a security team anywhere around, either.

"I don't like this," Gunn said at his elbow.

"What's the matter?" O'Flaherty said, from his

other side. He was as quiet as Gunn, faded into the shadows; Angel made a note to himself to ask Giles, someday, just what O'Flaherty did for the Watchers, back in the day. Not that it really mattered anymore.

"I can't hear anything except you," the vampire snapped. The humans fell silent, and O'Flaherty edged a wary step or two away.

Nothing.

Angel moved past the balcony, toward the front door.

Still nothing.

"Ah, the heck with it," he said, and ripped the door off its hinges.

Still nothing.

"Go," he said.

"Isn't that breaking and entering?" O'Flaherty inquired as he passed the vampire.

"We split the difference," Gunn explained. "He breaks, we enter."

"Make it fast," Angel said. "She'll have alarms."

Five minutes later:

"Nothing," Fred reported. "No Lilah's mom, no Lilah, no Izzaret, and definitely no book. The spell circle is still warm."

Angel heaved an entirely unnecessary—at least from the perspective of undead nonbreathingness—deep sigh. "All right. Plan B."

O'Flaherty stared at him. "You mean you're seriously—"

"Oh good, here's Lorne with another one of those little purple guys," Gunn interrupted.

"—going to invade Wolfram and Hart?"

"You had something else planned for the evening?"

He looks frantically around at his classmates. Across from him, Leslye-Flindshym has fainted; Haines is kneeling beside her. Davidowitz is scrunching his eyebrows together, trying to see; he realizes that Davidowitz does not realize there is a demon within killing distance.

On his other side, O'Flaherty trades him a sardonic, wry glance in exchange for his own terrified one. He would be shocked speechless at the other's courage if it were not for the way that O'Flaherty deliberately wipes the palms of his hands on his trousers to dry them. Somehow that helps, knowing that even O'Flaherty is terrified.

"Got any ideas, Head Boy?" O'Flaherty mouths, knowing that the creature below can hear even a whisper.

He opens his eyes wide, exaggerating helplessness. It is not exaggeration. O'Flaherty knows this.

"Not even one idea, Head Boy?" the vampire says.

They have just received a demonstration of just how acute vampire hearing is. And the thing's attention has now been attracted directly to them. It is laughing.

On his right side, Davidowitz edges away, trying to create distance between himself and the object of a vampire's attention. He succeeds only in attracting that attention.

"Oh, you're cute," the vampire says. "I've always liked boys with dark hair and blue blue eyes. They taste so good." Its hands flex; it crouches slightly. Davidowitz whimpers, and an acrid odor fills the room.

The vampire's nostrils wrinkle. "Oooo. Stinky." It pivots and leaps in one smooth movement to the opposite side of the room, and somehow it is up on the ledge with Leslye-Flindshym, and there is a spray of blood across the wall, and Haines has stumbled back, screaming.

She has not stumbled back far enough. The vampire backhands her, and she cartwheels through the railing and down three stories to land on her head and shoulder.

He had had a wet dream about Leslye-Flindshym last night.

Karrens is at one of the doors directly below him, trying desperately to force it open.

"Oh, please don't leave the party," the vampire says. "It's just beginning." It leaps over the railing again to the floor below and begins a slow advance on Karrens. Toward him.

"So if we're going to get out of here," Wesley went on as they jogged along in a random direction, "we're going to have to do it ourselves. We're going to have to come up with something new, aren't we? Which means finding out just how people have managed to survive so far, and use it against the thing."

"Oh, I say," Blanton said. He was slowing down already. "What makes you think you can do it when the rest of us haven't been able to?"

"Because I am *not* going to be reduced to nothing more than a paragraph in a book," Wesley said, looking him in the eye. "I'm not just going to read and run until it catches up with me."

"Oh, I say, that's rather harsh, isn't it?"

"Just how *have* you stayed alive so long, Blanton?"

"Well, quick wits, I like to think—"

"He pushes other people into its path," Matterdorf said spitefully. "I've seen him do it. It takes the first thing offered and he runs."

"You little bitch," Blanton said, but Wesley noticed he didn't bother to deny the accusation.

They had slowed to a walk now and were threading their way through broad stacks of newsprint.

"What do you do?" Wesley asked Matterdorf.

"I keep moving, go into new areas and rearrange things, shuffle them, mix them up. It slows the thing down, I've noticed—"

"Too much effort," Blanton muttered as he came around a corner and walked into the open jaws of the waiting Bookwyrm.

"We've scrambled the spells to the north," reported Gabriel, some time later. It was amazing how easily one got used to not telling time, Wesley thought. They had run while Blanton was being devoured. When they couldn't hear anymore, they'd stopped.

And they'd run, and escaped, and run again.

Wesley was more determined than ever to find a way out. He had sat down with Matterdorf and O'Flaherty and every other inhabitant of the book they could find, demanding that they continue the conversation, give him something to work from.

It was a conversation that had gone on for what, in another dimension, might have been days, or weeks. Wesley wanted to know every idea anyone had ever had, and where and how it had been tried out, and how well it had worked. And in the meantime he was trying to come up with ideas of his own.

Gabriel O'Flaherty was summarizing the actions he and some of the others had taken most recently. "Every third page is from a different text. N'gambo suggested introducing typographical errors—that's particularly effective in Latin, Swedish, and the African transliterations, we think. Those !Khoisan clicks can be simply disastrous in the wrong places."

Wesley nodded, hefting an ax in his hands. It was testing out the ideas, he'd found, that was the most difficult thing. What he had wasn't a particularly pretty weapon—papier-mâché transformed by an early Saxon spell into an iron battle-ax; he suspected there was something about the spells on the original paper that interfered with its taking any kind of an edge, but still, it was a weapon of a sort.

Unfortunately, the use of magick had drawn the Wyrm like a magnet. Blood still seeped from the wound in his arm where one of the antennae had caught him. He'd wrapped it with papyrus, to keep the blood for acting as a beacon to the thing as well.

But he had chopped it off—the first time, Gabriel told him later, that anyone could recall anyone in the book having actually hurt the Wyrm. The beast had screamed and vanished.

Shock, they decided later, because the next time, it had been willing to take much more damage before retreating. And it was clearly targeting Wesley now, its latest victims having fed it the information that he was the instigator of the rebellion in its realm. The diversionary tactics no longer worked. But now, at least, they had weapons, of a sort.

And what was more, it had learned new tricks itself in response to the organized resistance. It had taken to enthralling its victims. Wesley had seen people who had survived the Wyrm for decades sit still reading, oblivious, as the thing reared up over them. Even now, he could feel the urge to drop everything, to pick up something, anything, to find something new and interesting to read, as the Wyrm crawled through the page forest close by.

Something to get involved in. Distracted by.

"I've tried scuffing out a few lines, or marking through them where I can," Wesley said, very softly, trying to focus. "I'll run out of ink eventually, though. Can't scribble through too much."

"Oh, excellent idea. Although it's so painful to think of marking up books that way, isn't it?" Gabriel was fighting the impulse as well. "Oh look, the antenna grew back."

"Damn," Wesley said. It was true. The antenna had regenerated. "I wonder what it will take to kill it, then."

There was a small silence. Wesley thought Gabriel was probably shaking his head, mentally, at Wesley's conviction that the thing *could* be killed.

"What's it looking at?" Gabriel asked at last.

It was poised now a hundred yards away, rising up like a cobra preparing to strike, its antennae probing at the shuffled pages before it.

"I wrote several pages about the dual Slayers, Buffy and Faith. It seems to be fascinated."

O'Flaherty began to hum under his breath, *"And since it falls unto my lot,"* and despite himself, Wesley chuckled.

"Was a time, boy, you'd not have appreciated a good song or a good tale or a good beer," Gabriel said, interrupting himself. "You've had some fights since then."

"Yes," Wesley said quietly, not taking his eyes from the Wyrm.

"You've grown up."

"I suppose so," he said absently.

"Boys do. Even mine, bless his black heart. A true O'Flaherty, my Adrian always was. You never liked him, but he respected you, you know." The older man was swinging a wickedly hooked chain back and forth in one hand, running the other over a stack of spells beside him. "Ever since that final examination in the Testing Room."

Wesley almost turned to the older man to ask him about that, to tell him he had seen Adrian just before falling into the book, but something about the Wyrm caught his attention. The antennae, dozens of whips lashing from the head and jaws of the demon, were changing, thickening.

The ends were becoming knots. Knobs.

They were becoming new sets of jaws.

And the Wyrm was moving forward, snapping with all its mouths at once, hunting.

"Rutherford Circe," Lilah said, as she turned down the street to the Wolfram & Hart building.

The connection picked up almost instantly.

Almost, she thought cynically, as if he'd been waiting for her call.

"Yes?" That smooth BBC accent was really beginning to grate on her nerves.

"I believe I have something for you," she said. "That book you were interested in."

"Really?" The voice was a little less smooth, she noted. Interesting.

"Yes. Actually, I was thinking I might bring it by the office this evening—I have a few things in my office to clear up anyway. I could leave it there and you could pick it up in the morning—"

"No! No, that would be—I'm still in the office myself. Why don't I meet you here. In the Ancient Properties Archive. We can get it logged in immediately. Make sure it doesn't fall into the wrong hands."

Lilah slid to a stop at a red light and considered. Ever since she had looked up and seen Fred Burkle's huge brown eyes staring in at her through her patio door, she'd known that trouble was going to be hot on her heels. The little demon was on its own, but she'd taken the time to drop off her mother at the care facility. She hoped that hadn't cost her too much time.

As it was, one of her associates had turned up missing, and if that little weasel was the one who had tipped off Angel Investigations about the book, she was going to use his hide to give it a new cover. She hadn't even had a chance to look through the thing herself. If she took it to Ancient Properties for logging, she never *would* get a chance to examine it; logging it in would start the scanning process, reading it into Files and Records and the eidetic memory of Gwen, the secretary who *was* Files and Records and who held in her memory every single spell and secret filed away by Wolfram & Hart.

The light changed. As she crossed the intersection she glanced into the rearview mirror and saw only two cars and a city bus completing its last scheduled run for the night.

"Are you there, Ms. Morgan?" Circe was saying.

That black convertible turning onto the nearly empty street behind her looked uncomfortably familiar.

Damn.

"Yes, of course. I think that's an excellent idea, Mr. Circe. I'll meet you in the Ancient Properties Archive in ten minutes."

The Bookwyrm—a Bookhydra by now, Wesley thought—was diving and biting at him and Gabriel, taking chunks out of their flesh, lashing at them. The humans' weapons—quarterstaffs and whipping chains with wicked hooks attached to every link, and axes, dozens of axes, seemed to have no impact. They couldn't seem to scuff away the words before them anymore, and the effort wasn't slowing the beast down. The others trapped in the book were running alongside, striking at it, but the monster ignored them unless one got close enough to the multiple jaws to be snapped at; somewhere along the line Matterdorf had been caught in one of the larger mouths and was being swung over their heads, screaming.

Perhaps the amount of effort the thing had to put in to heave the overweight woman around like a rag doll in one of its newly created mouths was actually helpful. It was certainly dividing its attention. The other prisoners of the Compendium were beginning to be more successful in their efforts to harass the thing; the larger mouths focused on them. One of the many smaller mouths of the Bookwyrm descended on Gabriel's skull and began to chew at it.

Weakened by hours of battle and repeated wounds, Gabriel thrashed frantically but was unable to break free. Wesley swung his ax and severed the tentacle that had once been nothing more than an antenna, and ducked low to avoid another grasping set of teeth and pull the older man away.

But Gabriel wasn't there. Instead of moving with him, or even simply lying there bleeding, Gabriel was on his hands and knees, staring at the ground, reading the words written there. He was oblivious to the tangle of tentacles reaching for him and for Wesley; fascinated, enthralled, his finger traced the lines of the words before him. Wesley screamed in anger and frustration and skidded one foot along the line of text in front of the older man's foot just as one of the Wyrm's mouths grabbed him by the shoulder and tried to heave him into the air. He screamed again from the sudden shock of sucking agony, and Gabriel looked up, annoyed. The Wyrm lifted Wes off his feet, and he kicked out at Gabriel and caught him on the side.

Gabriel yelped, blinked, and rolled away from yet another mouth. He looked frantically up at Wesley, dangling inches above the printed ground, and then back to that same ground, yearningly.

"Gabriel!" Wesley yelled. "Fight it! It's mesmerizing you, *fight it*—"

With a desperate wail, Gabriel lunged for Wesley's ax and hacked at the tentacle holding him. The effort of his swing brought him facedown again on the ground, beside his own weapon, and he began to read again.

"Gabriel, no!"

The man jerked himself back up again to see Wesley lying a few feet away, struggling to pull himself up, the Wyrm raging, the words beckoning even through the sheen of blood beginning to cover them from the wounds on his own scalp, and his hands reached for the wickedly hooked chain.

There was a way, after all, to stop the words from luring him. To permanently stop them.

He wrapped the chain around his head. Tossed the end into one of the snapping mouths.

The mouth closed on the links, jerking back at the savage gouge of the hooks.

Gabriel shrieked and spun as the chain wrenched itself tight.

And the Wyrm disappeared, as if shocked itself at the breaking of its spell.

Wesley screamed again in protest, and even in his agony, Gabriel laughed. "Not a step I'm recommending, boyo, but don't you worry about me. We're mad, we Irish. Don't you know that by now? *I'll tell you a tale of peace and love—*"

I'll tell you a tale, Wesley thought as he pulled himself over to the older man, who sat now with the heels of his hands on his cheekbones, covering his ruined eyes. Another of his damned war songs. But—a tale.

A tale for a book. Like the tale of the two Slayers.

For a Bookwyrm.

A monster whose compulsion it is to read.

Who pulls the essence, the truth, of human lives out of them and spews them forth, creating a dimension as it goes.

Teller of tales, carrier of tales . . . who's going to carry the tale . . .

It was worth a try. Anything was, at this point. He dropped back and knelt by the bleeding Irishman.

He looks to his right, at Davidowitz. To his left, at O'Flaherty.

O'Flaherty, who has a penknife in his hand; a penknife with an absurdly small blade, and who is looking up, over their heads.

He measures distances with his eyes. The vampire has only to glance upward and will see the three of them on the ledge above Karrens. It has already demonstrated how easily it can jump so high.

He runs past O'Flaherty, around the circumference of the room, tries not to look at the body of Leslye-Flindshym, the gaping hole that is her throat. He grasps one of the broken banisters and pulls with all his strength, tearing it loose. The vampire looks around at the sound of cracking wood.

It is not heavy enough to penetrate dead bone, if thrown. It needs muscle behind it. He reaches down and breaks another banister free, the only other piece that is available, and swallows hard. "Ms. Karrens!" he calls. "Here!"

He throws one of the makeshift stakes. It falls short. The vampire stares at it, and at him, incredulously. It makes no move to come forward, to pick up the stake. Of course it wouldn't; a vampire has no need for a stake.

He risks a glance straight across. It is ready, he thinks. He hopes. But not unless the vampire is in place.

"Render any assistance you feel advisable."

This is not advisable. This is madness. He is depending on the ingenuity of someone he loathes. But if he does not try, who knows how many more of them will die before random chance will bring the thing where it must be?

He steps back into the winding stairway. Goes down the stairs. Opens the thin, wooden door. Walks steadily into the middle of the Testing Room.

Faces the Vampire.

Lilah had pulled a lot of all-nighters in the offices of Wolfram & Hart; slipping the passkey through the slot, slapping her palm against the ID pad was automatic. Similarly, she was also used to running in high heels, although at least this time she wasn't in spikes.

"Security! Code Yellow!" she yelled as she ran through the lobby.

Instantly, the guard on night duty, a Taggit demon, whipped out a cell phone and started lumbering in her wake.

"Code Yellow," the Taggit repeated into the phone. "Head of Special Projects. We're"—he looked up to see Lilah's direction—"heading for the elevators."

A Code Yellow meant something big was in hot

pursuit; prepare to intercept and destroy. The Taggit demon looked nervously around the deserted lobby and started after her.

Lilah had gotten there well ahead of him. She wasn't about to wait for the Taggit to get its seven-hundred-plus pounds into motion; as the door slid shut, she yelled back at him, "Ancient Properties! Get it in gear, or you'll never have another clutch!"

Sagging against the back of the elevator, she pressed the book to her chest. Then, remembering the surveillance cameras, she straightened up again. There was no point in letting the tapes show her as anything but self-possessed, in perfect control at all times.

It was tough, panting when in perfect control.

She reminded herself to get more hours in the gym. This was silly. A little sprint like that shouldn't have winded her. She'd done a ten-miler only two days ago.

There had better be a team waiting for her, or she'd have a Taggit-hide rug in her office tomorrow.

She looked down at the book in her arms. It itched.

Maybe she could stop somewhere and copy that spell. It wouldn't be so hard to find—just open to the Contents page and skim—

The elevator door slid open just as she shifted the book in her arms.

A full security squad was arrayed before her, weapons out and pointing in her direction.

Perfect control at all times, she reminded herself, and raised one elegant eyebrow. "Thanks for the welcoming committee," she said, stepping forward. Two black-clad guards with AK-47s gave way before her. "You can escort me the rest of the way. They're not that far behind me."

She led the way at a fast walk, two of the six squad members acting as point men ahead and to either side of her, two more in front, the last two behind.

The circle of highly trained killers, sworn to guard her with her life, should have made her feel more secure. Being inside the wards and protections of the Los Angeles branch of Wolfram & Hart should have made her feel more secure. Why didn't she feel more secure?

She'd never realized how far it really was to the Ancient Properties wing. She had to pass the dormitory where the Seers slept, the laboratory where they gave up their muddy clairvoyant visions; the Archives, where all the reference books were stored; Files and Records, with the never-sleeping clerk Gwen, who could access everything in the Archives as fast as she could formulate the question; the intersecting hallways that led to even more esoteric areas.

Gwen—of course! This book would end up in the Archives; she could ask Gwen about the spell.

Of course, the senior partners, and any unscrupulous employee of the firm, could then ask Gwen what she'd been after. That was a drawback.

Perhaps she'd borrow one of the Templates. That way, she could read the book herself without having to get it out of the Archives. She didn't think the Templates, the blank books that reflected any book in the Archives on request, kept an actual record of what was requested.

Of course, she'd have to come up with a good reason to need a Template.

The brisk tapping of her heels against the steel floor reflected the hammering of her heart. She walked faster, and almost overran her point men.

She wanted to get rid of this thing, suddenly, much more than she wanted to read it. Even finding the spell that would restore her mother's mind wasn't worth this. For some reason Angel's people were after this thing, and while she didn't fear Angel *more* than the senior partners, she didn't want to antagonize him unnecessarily either.

She'd turn this in, and then they'd have to get off her back. She could go back to her day-to-day work in peace and quiet and figure out a way to get rid of the vampire with a soul without the threat of actually confronting him. Angel was supposed to have a role in the coming Apocalypse, and the senior partners wanted him alive for that. She didn't care, in this one case, what the senior partners wanted. If she had anything to say about it, Angel would be dead long before any Apocalypse happened. Nobody who made her feel this scared had any business living. Or being undead, anyway.

Somewhere in the building, an alarm sounded.

She walked faster. The security detail fingered their weapons and cleared hallways before they'd let her pass.

The alarm cut off. False positive? She doubted it.

There, at the end of the passage, where it intersected another corridor. That was the entrance to the Ancient Properties wing, a metal door engraved with protective runes, an Eye of Horus over the top of it all. The door was standing ajar.

And thank the Powers of Evil, there was Rutherford Circe, waiting behind a semicircle of black-clad security. Smiling with relief, she stepped forward to hand him the book.

"We'll take that," Angel said.

"What are you thinking?" Gabriel asked, moving his face sightlessly to the sounds of Wesley moving. His face was still covered in dried blood. One hand was touching lightly at the blood; the other clutched at the pages on which he lay.

Wesley had pulled the older man back into the trees. Behind them, they could hear—nothing.

The Wyrm had disappeared again. Gabriel was lying on the ground, still pale with shock and pain. Wesley had tried to wipe the blood away, but the head wound would not stop seeping.

"The Wyrm reads, you said," Wesley reminded him, standing up to pace. "It makes this world so it can write us.

"What if we write something for it to create?"

"What do you mean? Write—a fiction? We're scientists of magick, young man. We do not write *fiction*. I wouldn't know how." He lay back with a grunt and a sigh.

"I would," Wesley said. He fumbled in his shirt pocket for his pen.

"What would you write?" Gabriel asked. One hand reached out, trembling, to touch a sheaf of pages.

"We'll spin it a tale," Wesley said.

"The words won't stay. Even when we changed the spells, they changed back. Only the Wyrm's words—our lives—stay the same."

Wesley swallowed hard. "Well then, we'll just have to convince it that it's telling the tale itself. And make sure it's there to read it when I write it. If I manage it—can you distract it long enough?"

Gabriel was silent for a long, long moment. When he spoke, he didn't bother to point out the obvious. He could no longer see to avoid the monster. "What I miss, you know. I can't see this." His fingers ruffled the pages again. "You're mad. It'll eat us both."

"Not if—if I move fast enough. All we have to do is keep ahead of it long enough to let me write. I'll start, and if you help me—if you call it—"

"With my blood," Gabriel said. "Since it wants to devour us, it should be looking for me. I'm bleeding enough."

Wesley swallowed. "Yes. I'll tell it that—that there's an exit. That we can go back, and we'll take it to—to the mother lode of books. Someplace that would put everything you know from the Council Library to shame."

"There is no such place," Gabriel said indignantly.

Wesley sighed. "That's why they call it fiction. But it may be fooled long enough that it will actually create the exit as it reads."

"It will know it's a lie."

"Maybe it won't realize it. It's not used to reading actual fiction, after all. You haven't tried this before, have you?"

"No, of course not."

"Well then, let's *try*, at least."

Gabriel's blind face moved with him as he paced, following the sound of his footsteps as a flower follows the sun. After a moment a pained smile escaped from him, however unwilling. "I've seen this before in you, you know. You managed it then. Do you remember?"

"I don't think I do," Wesley said uncertainly. "I don't know—"

"I do. I remember. And who knows, perhaps you'll do it now, too. Stand up before us all and save the day. I'm sorry I won't be able to read your fiction. I'm sure it will be quite wonderful.

"All right, Mr. Wyndam-Pryce. Let's give it a try, shall we? You'll have to carry me out there. So let's get to it."

The odds could have been better, Angel considered. On his side, two women, pretty good with their weapons but hardly trained to expert level. One former Watcher of dubious loyalties. Gunn, whose recovery from the Tovateir poison was nearly complete. And himself, of course.

On the other—two full squads of Wolfram & Hart security, trained, armed to the teeth.

Well, the odds could have been worse, too.

They had already taken out the first level of security, which guarded the service entrance to the basement level. Now a demon guard responded to Angel's statement by raising the AK-47—a stupid move, in Angel's estimation; you didn't want to use automatic weapons when a department head was in your line of fire.

Cordelia took him out with a blast from a shotgun.

"Nice," Fred said as she took out two more with volleys from her own, cut-down weapon. "Where'd you learn that?"

"Shooting skeet on a cruise," Cordelia responded, taking aim at the next guard as the rest of them moved into action. "You?"

"Rabbits on my cousin's farm," Fred assured her hastily as she blew off another demon's head. It was amazing how blasé one could become about fighting demons after a while.

Meanwhile, Angel opted for the direct approach, driving straight for the book in Lilah's hands. Seeing him coming, she ducked back behind Circe.

"Looks like some cutting-off-ness is in order," Cordy said.

"Cutting," Fred responded, and moved back to fire at the doorway. Lilah nearly walked into the hail of buckshot, and reversed her course abruptly. The older man in the suit caught some of the ricochet and cried out.

His voice was lost in the full-throated roar Angel gave as he let the demon out.

Angel tore through the first two guards, not even giving them time to aim before he threw the first into the second, sending them both sprawling into the wall. Behind him, Gunn used a bo stick in close quarters, punching one man under the breastbone and knocking another up the side of the head. As he did so, another guard, one of the demons, came up behind him and aimed a gun at his shaved skull. Gunn heard the click as the slide came back, and spun around only to see O'Flaherty sliding a knife into the demon's guts. It screamed and wobbled. The gun fired, but instead of hitting its intended target, it took out another of the guards.

Gunn nodded thanks and went back to battle.

The first two that Angel hit had managed to pull themselves together and try to get back into the fight. They threw themselves on Angel together, bearing him down to the floor.

Normally, two human beings couldn't keep a vampire down. But one of these was a Takhesh demon, and it was *heavy*. He twisted underneath the demon, trying to avoid the stake it had pulled from a side holster, while the other tried to hold him still.

He could reach out and grab the human, snap at him, tear his throat out, with no effort at all.

He couldn't.

The Takhesh was holding down his arms now. The human grabbed the stake and held it high, preparing to plunge it into Angel's heart.

He sagged, as if defeated.

Sure enough, the Takhesh let up the pressure, and he twisted, wrapping his legs around the human and throwing him across the room. The Takhesh scrambled to recover, and Angel jerked his head up, catching the demon under the chin. He could hear the demon's fangs crack together, and it grunted in pain and lifted its hands in reflex.

It was all Angel needed. He pushed upward and

outward, and the Takhesh's hold broke. In an instant, Angel was on his feet again, snatching up the human's discarded stake and shoving it deep into the Takhesh's brain.

He didn't stop to watch the demon die— Takhesh didn't dust or dissolve, they just lay there. He spun around to take on the next opponent.

But there was no next opponent. Angel's yellow-eyed gaze skimmed the room. The dozen guards were on the floor in disarray. Fred and Cordelia were favoring injuries, but were still poised in case one of the recumbent bodies moved.

Lilah Morgan was looking at the wreck of Wolfram & Hart security with complete disgust.

Gunn was holding an old, battered book in one hand and a cigarette lighter in the other. The flame danced within an inch of the cover. Angel could smell the leather cover singeing.

The vampire shook his head, and restored his human face.

"Gunn?" he said cautiously. "Is that—"

"Always did want to see what book-burning was all about," Gunn said. His chest was still heaving from the exertion of the fight.

"No!" Dabet, Lorne, Circe, Fred, Cordy, Lilah, and Angel replied in ragged chorus.

And there was another voice too. Standing in the hallway behind him, just behind Lorne and Dabet, was a teenage boy. At least, he *thought* it was a boy;

the kid's face and hands were streaked with red-gold lines squirming under the skin like so many nightcrawlers. His face was preternaturally pale in the spaces between the lines.

"No," the kid repeated. "Don't burn it, don't, it's a book—" He staggered forward two strides and then stopped, as if having trouble keeping himself on his feet.

Angel blinked. Who the hell was *this*?

At least Lorne was here, with the little book collector at his side; Dabet was yearning toward the book in Gunn's hand, as if he wanted to run across the room and climb up his body to it.

"Why not?" Gunn demanded. "Seems to me that burnin' this damned thing might be the quickest way of getting whatever's in there out—"

A babble of protest—and O'Flaherty said, above it all, "We brought the Izzaret to open the thing, none of the rest of us can read it—"

"I'll read it!" the kid said. He stumbled forward. "Give it to me, I'll take it, I'll use it—"

He grabbed at the book in Gunn's hand. In the process, the cigarette lighter was thrust against the ancient leather.

The stink of burning hide filled the air. Gunn shoved the kid to the floor.

Flames licked up the book's spine.

Dabet screamed in panic at the sight of one of his precious books burning, and launched himself at Gunn, the book, and the kid, fanged jaws agape and claws ripping at the air.

Cordy threw a battle-ax across the room and cut the little demon in half before he got ten feet. "There," she said, cold-eyed. "One less to worry about."

Nice move, Angel thought, approving. He'd always known Cordelia had a spine of solid steel. She also had excellent aim.

"And so much for our ability to get into the book ourselves," Adrian O'Flaherty pointed out acerbically. "Or getting someone out."

The book was burning fiercely now, enveloped in flames. Gunn dropped it next to the kid, who reached for it and yelped as his striped hands encountered fire.

Ouch, Angel thought. That *was* why they'd brought the little demon along, after all. *Oops. Now what?*

"Perhaps you don't *want* everything that's in there to get out," Circe said. "Have you considered that possibility?"

"We want Wesley out," Fred said. She was holding the shotgun steady at the few guards still moving. "We want Wesley back."

Charles Gunn gave her a long look. "Yeah," he said at last. "What she said. How do we get him out of here—if this is really where he is? Because I'm tellin' you, if he comes back from a trip up the coast tomorrow . . ."

"We needed an Izzaret," O'Flaherty said hoarsely.

His left arm hung useless—broken—at his side. He leaned over the dead Dabet, and, picking up the battle-ax from the gore of the dead book collector, he walked up to Circe. "Or do we?"

All eyes were on the former Watcher now, the Watcher and Wolfram & Hart's Head Librarian.

Very deliberately, O'Flaherty wiped the blade clean on the front of Circe's suit, leaving a smear of darker blue gore on the blue suit.

Lilah Morgan edged away, opening up as much distance between herself and the Librarian as she could.

Circe stared at O'Flaherty, speechless.

O'Flaherty set the blade of the ax under the older man's chin. "I'm going to do this," he says softly. "Now or later. I don't really care which. So it's your choice. Can you open the book for them before it turns completely to ashes?"

"I don't think that's going to happen," Fred muttered. "It's burning, but it's not being consumed. Look."

Only Fred and the kid were looking at the book, though. The rest of them were watching the two men standing in the doorway of the Ancient Properties wing.

"Who *are* you?" Circe demanded. "What's this about?"

"Look me in the eye and tell me you don't remember O'Flaherty," Adrian suggested, gently pressing the battle-ax blade against the man's throat.

"O'Flaherty?" Circe looked confused. "O'Flaherty? He was the Council's—you—you're his son?"

"Oh, excellent. You *do* remember. Although I'm told it's a strong family resemblance."

"But I don't understand—"

"You ought to. You killed him."

"Aha!" Cordelia whispered out of the side of her mouth to Fred and Angel. "I *knew* that guy had an agenda."

But Circe was still staring at Adrian. "What are you talking about?"

"I've been looking for you," the other man said between his teeth. "You were seen leaving the Library just before the explosion, just before the building collapsed. They tried to call my father up to the Council meeting. But he wasn't there, was he?

"They saw you leaving. Carrying an armload of books. He'd never let you remove books from the Library, would he?

"He was dead before the rest of them. You killed him.

"I should have guessed you'd end up here. Did you use the Council's books to buy your way in?"

"Actually, I think he did," Lilah said. "We'd been in negotiations for a long time, as I recall. He said he was going to bring us the best of the Council's collection." She looked at the book. It was burning even more brightly now, even hotter, the pages fanned out and still whole. The kid was still trying to grab hold of it, whimpering.

"Lilah!" Circe said.

"Well, there had to be some justification for that salary. But you killed the Librarian?" She smiled. "That's more initiative than we expected."

"But I—"

Adrian cursed, and swung the ax out with his good arm to strike.

"Wait!" Fred cried out. "Don't—Wesley—"

Angel launched himself across the room, ready to throw himself into the path of the ax if necessary.

He had just grabbed O'Flaherty's arm when there was a massive flash of light.

When they could see again, a bleeding Wesley and an older man with ruined eyes were staggering from their knees before them, and a gaping dimensional vortex loomed overhead. The boy looked straight up into it and laughed.

"Wesley!" Fred and Cordelia shrieked.

Adrian O'Flaherty cried out too.

"Get back! Get him out of the way!" Wesley yelled. "It's following us!"

And the Bookwyrm began to emerge from the vortex behind them and head directly for the open doorway of Ancient Properties and Rutherford Circe, with Adrian O'Flaherty between them. It did not appear to notice the boy, also in its path.

Angel dove at the massive demon. He hit the rounded gray side and slid off, rolling away from the scrabbling legs.

Cordelia began firing steadily at the Bookwyrm. Fred picked up her shotgun again and did likewise.

The Wyrm was still half-in, half-out of the vortex. There wasn't room for it in the corridor in front of the Ancient Properties wing.

Angel picked himself up and ran to pull O'Flaherty Senior out of the way of the thrashing legs. Wesley took over and dragged the man into the side corridor. The Wyrm roared and whipped its head around, into a hail of buckshot, and pulled back a bit. Adrian O'Flaherty ran to his father's side.

Angel snarled, vamped out again, and leaped to the top of the Wyrm's head, smashing at it with Cordelia's battle-ax.

The Wyrm screamed, trying to retreat. But there was no retreating from the demon on its head. It lifted itself as far as it could, trying to smash the vampire against the ceiling. Angel dropped flat and slid down on its neck, hanging on only by the haft of the ax buried in the thing's head. The blast of shotguns—and automatic rifles, when the women were out of shells—crashed and echoed in the corridor. The Wyrm's multiple legs scrambled and tossed the bodies of the Wolfram & Hart security squads as it lashed its body back and forth, farther and farther out of the vortex.

"It's not dying," Gunn said in disbelief. "Damn. That thing isn't dying."

"And it's not stopping," Cordelia added, throwing down a weapon and picking up another. "It's not even slowing down!"

"It's the book," Gabriel said. "Have to get the book."

Across the recumbent form of his father's body, Adrian O'Flaherty looked at Wesley Wyndam-Pryce and grinned. "Well then," he said. "We've done this before, now haven't we? Playing hare and hounds? Only this time it's my turn to play the rabbit—"

"What the devil are you talking about—"

But O'Flaherty was on his feet already, back in the corridor, back to where the Wyrm was shoving more and more of itself through the vortex. Circe and Lilah had run into the Ancient Properties wing and were trying to close the door against the pressure of bodies being pushed against it. Fred and Cordelia, Lorne and Gunn had retreated as far as they could. All of them had taken up weapons and were firing steadily. It seemed to have no effect. As O'Flaherty came up to them, they put up the muzzles to keep from hitting him.

Looks up to locate O'Flaherty and nearly falls

*before the vampire's rush; but even as he is retreat-
ing, he realizes that O'Flaherty has sawn through the
curtain cord, and blinding sunlight has fallen across
the parquet floor, and the vampire has transformed
from ravening demon into writhing mass of flames
and an explosion of dust that covers him, coats him.
He can taste it, taste the flavor of Vampire.*

"Oh, bloody idiot," Wesley said, and followed
him. "You fool! It follows blood! It's not going to
pay any attention to you!"

O'Flaherty gave him a hard, tight grin as he
skidded to a stop in front of the monster. "Is that
so, then? Come on, Pryce. One for the dear old
Watchers Academy. Come on, Head Boy!"

With that, he stooped down and pulled a combat
knife out of the boot of one of the dead guards.
Facing the wounded Wyrm, he yelled, "Blood, is
it? I'll give you blood!" He slashed with the knife,
opening up his shirt and spreading a torrent of
crimson across his chest. "I'll give you blood, damn
you! Here! Blood! Taste it!"

The Wyrm roared and squeezed around to face
him, its antennae reaching for him, for the blood.

Wesley ran to the thing's side, searching desperately. But the kid—the kid without a name, with
lines of demonic infection in his veins—finally had
grabbed the Compendium, clutching it like a
teddy bear.

The Wyrm swung around to face them both,

O'Flaherty and the child. It rose up, its main mouth stretching wide, and fell.

The boy, holding the book, was engulfed.

Adrian O'Flaherty leaped for the exposed eyes, stabbing.

The Wyrm shuddered. A ripple went down its body, as if it were a long throat, swallowing. The mouth opened again, pulsed. The antennae jaws snapped, crowding at O'Flaherty, and then froze.

The Wyrm retched, as if trying to rid itself of its last meal.

It whimpered.

Convulsed.

"Angel!" Wesley yelled, his voice hoarse.

Angel scrambled up the haft of the battle-ax, wrenched it loose, and swung it in a wide, horizontal strike, taking off the Wyrm's antennae.

The gray, massive demon screamed, a high, thin tone that made the metal walls quiver, and it twisted.

The book came back up, the flames doused at last, and fell underneath the Wyrm.

Wesley ducked in and pried loose the book from under the weight of the thing's body. The Wyrm rolled back, and he slipped in the blood. The demon rolled the other way, toward him.

Angel heaved up the battle-ax again and drove it into the side of the demon's gaping mouth.

Gunn pulled Wesley back.

The Wyrm kept gagging, retching, convulsing.

Adrian O'Flaherty staggered along the wall, leaving smears of blood as he went.

"Hey, there!" he called. "Head Boy!"

Wesley, clutching the book, looked up.

O'Flaherty threw the knife across the room, and collapsed.

Wesley picked it up and started hacking at the Red Compendium.

It came to pieces in his hands.

The boards of the book splintered. Wesley opened it and slashed, over and over. For Artie, and Tobey, and Blanton, and all the rest, for the unknown boy the Wyrm could not consume, the blade of the knife rose and fell until the pages were confetti, soaked in blood, unreadable. The demon rose up once more, screaming.

Angel hacked again with the battle-ax, and the Bookwyrm's head fell apart.

EPILOGUE

"Do we know who the kid was yet?" Angel asked two days later, as they walked out of the hospital.

"Yeah," Cordelia said. "The same one I saw in that vision about the high school lab. He was Emilio Herrera. His father worked for Wolfram and Hart. Say no more."

"Did you see how the Wyrm reacted to him? Emilio, I mean? Wes thinks the kid was infected by those little demons. He thinks the infection poisoned the Wyrm, at least enough to slow it down." Fred shuddered.

"I'm surprised Wes could see the kid well enough to tell," Cordy muttered. "He'd lost his glasses, after all."

Angel pulled the rim of the fedora down tight against the setting sun. It wasn't quite safe for him to expose himself to the outside yet.

"I wasn't seeing *anything*," Cordelia went on.

"I'm still trying to understand how someone could put out his own eyes."

"Wes said he had to, to stop reading inside the book. There wasn't any other way. He's a brave man." Angel stepped into the parking elevator with relief, leading the way to the GTX.

"His son, too," Fred agreed. "But that's what I mean. He did that—that awful thing to himself, to prevent himself from reading and falling under the spell of anything like the Bookwyrm again. But—"

"No buts," Angel said firmly. "For a man like that, it's the ultimate sacrifice."

"I guess so," Fred said, getting into the front seat.

But she couldn't shake the image of their last farewell, at the elevator in the hospital. Adrian O'Flaherty, his chest wrapped in layers of bandages, was saying farewell to Wesley. His father, his eyes heavily bandaged, stood by.

And as Adrian turned away, the older man's hand touched the call button, and dropped down. She would never forget the look on Gabriel O'Flaherty's face as his fingertips discovered the raised dots of Braille beneath the buttons—the look of wonder and despair and utter relief on the ruined face as Gabriel O'Flaherty realized that, despite everything, he could *still read. . . .*

Seven of the surviving members of the sixth form, plus the Watcher Gillie Karrens, formally request a complete Cleansing of their memories before the end of the day. Out of all of the members of this class, only two will graduate from the Watchers Academy, having successfully passed the Practical Examination. Their names are Wesley Wyndam-Pryce and Adrian O'Flaherty.

ABOUT THE AUTHOR

Ashley McConnell is the author of more than a dozen fantasy, horror, and media novels. Her first book, *Unearthed,* was a finalist for the Bram Stoker Award. She lives in Albuquerque, New Mexico, with three cats, two dogs, and two Morgan horses, all of whom want dinner at exactly the same time.